# THE RELUCTANT
# DETECTIVE

**Kiran Manral** is a freelance writer, blogger and media consultant who lives in Mumbai with her family. She is also the founder of India Helps, a volunteer network which works with disaster victims.

westland ltd
61, II Floor, Silverline Building, Alapakkam Main Road, Maduravoyal, Chennai 600095
93, I Floor, Sham Lal Road, Daryaganj, New Delhi 110002

First published in India by westland ltd 2011

Copyright © Kiran Manral 2011

10 9 8 7 6 5 4 3 2

ISBN: 978-93-81626-11-5

Typeset by Arun Bisht

# THE RELUCTANT
# DETECTIVE

*Or how a housewife became
a murder investigator between
being a school-gate mom
and her ladies lunches*

## Kiran Manral

*w*

# CHAPTER 1

# IN WHICH THERE IS NEVER ANYTHING TO WEAR

I ADJUSTED THE STRAP OF MY TRIPLE-SUPPORT harness-like bra, cleverly designed to defy the dictates of gravity, and got back to the task of figuring out a suitable ensemble for the situation. The T-shirt I had on—faded into an indeterminate colour—was just temporary. I had exactly an hour to make myself glamorous—a task that would daunt movie stars, let alone a lesser mortal like me.

I was headed to a party. Don't get me wrong; I have done my fair share of partying, but this was in youthful days when harnesses were not required and you could spin a top on the tummy aka Kamal Hassan in *Ek Duje Ke Liye*, so one could basically drag on sack cloth and ashes and rock the look.

I rifled through my wardrobe with the mounting panic that comes from realising that whatever you own and is suitable for partying of the highest order is a) too tight b) totally out of style, as the time since I've bought party clothes, or have had need of party clothes has been close on five years or c) has holes in it from the silverfish that have been diligently gnawing away over the past so many years. Party invitations should not be snuck on you when you're at your lowest premenstrual bloated self, with the errant sebaceous eruption on the tip of your nose. No, invitations to such dos should be handed over weeks, even months, in advance, so you can plan your look down to the last artificial beauty spot on your face. And of course have enough spare time to get your hair set, and coordinate your nail polish with the outfit you will no doubt run out and buy especially for the occasion. Because, of course, there is never anything to wear in your wardrobe.

An introduction is in order at this stage. I am Kay. Kanan Mehra. Gold. Bred of the fire of a furnace. Although Mumbai in June, my birth month, would qualify for the position easily. Kanan, thankfully without the addition of the Bala that plagues most other Kanans of the female gender I have known. I associate Kananbala with Lalu Prasad Yadav, for his unfortunate circumstance of having them tufts of white hair emanating from his ears.

I am a thirty-five-year-old, mother of a five-year-old, housewife. Okay, okay, I may not be a typical stay-at-home housewife, with a penchant for keeping the house immaculate, whipping up Cordon Bleu recipes and happy to have guests come over at the drop of a hat. In fact, I am barely home. I'm busy. I keep myself busy. I must be the only Cancerian on this planet whose nesting instincts involve the chucking out of old, and ergo been seen in public, garbs to make space for the new in the wardrobe. Speaking of which, the husband is grumbling about three shelves in his section being usurped by my things which have taken on a life of their own and are multiplying at a rate made popular by the very sexually active populace of the single-celled life form known by those who actually make bread and cake, as yeast.

To come back to the moment of crisis. Party-time looming large. When I say large, I mean really large and imminent. As in, within an hour. And no ordinary party this. This was a party of gigantic proportions, at which film stars and models and beautiful people would no doubt be present. A party also known as 'a do'. Supposedly to celebrate the success of a movie that featured a couple of Bollywood's hottest stars. Why had we been invited? The spouse is a nodding acquaintance of one of the chappies who co-produced it, via a close friend. Who is the spouse's chaddi buddy. And therefore it was mandatory for the spouse to attend, although we were of the antisocial variety on regular days. I would probably need to take along a little rock to hide behind. Make that a boulder.

I scanned the contents of my colour-coded wardrobe quickly. Blue suede trousers and cropped jacket? I might have to snip away inches of cellulite to get into it. Black Next skinny fits with spaghetti strap top with nice frill at the neck. I might end up looking unbalanced and ready to topple over with a slight push from a single finger. Flowing kaftany top, with Pucci print over aforementioned Next skinny fits and worn with improbably high heels. I might just get a crystal ball handed to me at a table, be forced to read the fortunes of party guests, and not be allowed to charge for the same. I flopped down in despair into the huge armchair that I keep right next to the wardrobe for moments just like this. The son wandered in, a Power Ranger action figure in his hand that was on the verge of being dismembered in a cruel manner.

Kabir, aka the brat, is the handsomest five-year-old tyke in the entire world and I dare you to challenge that. He is also undoubtedly in the category that kind souls call spirited and unkind souls call hyperactive. He settled down on the bed with the expectant air of a show about to begin, and wanting to grab ringside seats.

'Mamma, wear d black pant,' he said in a tone that conveyed that the matter was now settled.

'Why, darling?' I asked. 'Does Mamma look nice in the black pant?'

He shook his head vaguely to indicate a no. 'I wantu see you pud it on.'

The pant in question is a skinny fit. I, in question, am not a skinny or fit. Therefore the putting on process is one that entails a lot of huffing and puffing, and pulling in of belly, and wriggling on the ground, and ensuring all visits to the bathroom are dealt with before one puts a toe into said skinny fit, or endure the humiliation of holding oneself in for the entire duration of the evening, rather than risk visiting the restroom for fear of not being able to get the two sides of the zipper to cooperate and merge back together as they should.

As entertaining as it might be for the son, it was not sufficient for Mamma to accept the suggestion, and the hunt continued. I fished out a pair of off-white linen drawstring pants, with a coordinated tunic top that fitted just enough to show the remnants of a waistline without me getting into the mutton-masquerading-as lamb area. Elegant enough, I thought, without me having to spend the evening afraid to exhale. But would it be considered appropriate to wear linen to an evening do?

'Den, whachyur wearing?' Kabir persisted, with the curiosity that comes from knowing that, for Mamma, every dress-up occasion is cause for much angst and tantrum-throwing.

'I don't know, love,' I replied in the distracted way I have when all the contents of my wardrobe of the party wear variety are spread out on the bed, and nothing seems to work.

I decided to check what the spouse was wearing and take inspiration from him. He is a sensible and practical man, a no-frills retrosexual male who is dressed to party if he is wearing a shirt and a pair of trousers and shoes, never mind current fashion trends. If he's in a good mood, he will even shave. Occasionally he looks down to check if his socks match. It saves time in front of the mirror during the get-ready rush before a party.

The spouse was slipping into a most appealing moss green linen shirt, with light blue jeans and his regular white sneakers. Freshly showered, he looked good enough to eat. I thought this was grossly unfair given he had put in absolutely no effort, and complained vocally about it.

'You're ready already? I haven't even decided what to wear,' I said, hopping around in the agony of indecision, a hopping around rivalled in agony only by the hopping around of one in urgent need to go to a bathroom and not being in the vicinity of one.

I pulled out the remaining strands of my hair, which were still just that wee bit damp from the shower, and went back to deciding what to wear. The child lost interest and wandered off.

'Mamma,' he called over his shoulder. 'Is only clothes. Wear anything.'

From the mouth of one who was a zygote in my uterus once upon a time, this indictment stung. I picked up the first thing that came to hand, which was a copper-brown, light weave top, in a wrap-around style. I had copper shoes to go with it, a perfect rip-off of an LV pair I had seen adorning the feet of them beautiful people; delicately strappy with the motif part of the design bang in the centre of the foot. Lovely. But the toes needed post-box red nail polish to carry it off.

I am nothing if not determined, so I got down to the task at hand with nail polish remover, cotton and a bottle of post-box red nail paint. Then I looked at the clock and the growing storm on the spouse's face as he saw me still in a state of flagrante undressio, and said damn the nail polish remover, and slathered on the red on top of the pale pink that already existed.

Applying nail polish is an art. You need non-shaky hands. And a calm and Zen-like nature. I am not calm and have but a nodding acquaintance with Zen. At the best of times, I'm not great at applying nail polish, and if anyone has attempted to apply nail polish when they are in a rush, they will understand the difficulties involved. Your hands will shake. Your hands will take the nail polish beyond the boundaries of your nail and onto the surrounding skin, you will carefully loop it off your skin with a handy ear bud, only to realise you have now got it onto your fingernails, which were also pale pink to begin with, but will now have to be made post-box red—you could never live down the indignity of mottled red and pink nail polish that looks like the visage of a rabid dog, and will spend the entire evening holding your hand petulantly behind your back and refusing to extend it even when you are being introduced to folk you cannot air-kiss and must shake hands with, aka senior corporate types.

So I hastily finished the feet and got started on the fingernails. The child wandered in again, a cup of milk in his hands, and his face lit up at the sight of the discarded red ear buds on the bed.

'Mamma,' he squeaked gleefully, 'your ears is blooding? Lemme see!!! Lemme see!!!'

He clambered over me, trying to get a peek into the offending orifice, hoping to see rivers of blood flowing out. He's at the age where blood is the most fascinating thing; thankfully, this stage doesn't last beyond eight. I hope. If he's still tearing wings off butterflies at eight, I will need to be very, very worried.

He peered into my ear, pulling at the earlobe with the kind of frenetic innocence that just begs for a smack (which I would have administered gently, of course, for all ye democratic parenting advocates out there), but I desisted, given that the nail paint was still drying. Very slowly.

'Whachyure wearing now?' Kabir squeaked and picked up the off-white pair of linen trousers I'd laid out carefully on the bed, with hands that had just a few minutes ago made close acquaintance with a bar of melted chocolate.

I flew at him, grabbed said trousers back to safety (managing to keep my nail polish smudge-free in the process) and threatened him with a curfew on park playing time if he didn't leave the room NOW, and let me dress in peace.

He sauntered out and settled himself on the sofa in the drawing room. In a few seconds, I heard the opening strains of *Oggy and the Cockroaches* rumbling like seismic sound waves through the floor and walls of the home. 'Switch the home theatre off,' I yelled, sticking a head out from behind the door.

As I closed the door shut, I heard, through the vibrations of the laughter of cockroaches, the intercom buzzing. My maid, closer to the instrument than I was, answered, and had a two-minute conversation that ended with the intercom being slammed down. 'Bhabhiiiiiii, Bhabhiiiiii,' she yelled. Jamuna yells as a matter of course, and would have yelled even if said door had been wide open.

'Kya hua?' I asked, again sticking my head out from behind the door. Maybe the sky really had finally fallen down, given the urgency of her summons. 'Bhabhi, the police are downstairs. They're asking for you.'

Needless to say, all thoughts of getting into copper top and rip-off LV stilettos were discarded hastily, and I hauled myself back into the discarded tracks and tee and ran out into the living room. And noted that I had smudged my carefully-applied red polish.

# CHAPTER 2

# CLOSE ENCOUNTERS WITH THE POLICE KIND

**I** WALKED INTO THE LIVING ROOM TO find the front door open and Jamuna peeping into the passage leading to the elevators, with a look on her face that hovered between curiosity and fear.

The elevator doors chimed and opened, and the disembodied voice with an accent that was anywhere between Japanese and the American Midwest announced the floor. Two policemen in the dull khaki that the government has decreed will be the colour of the diligent hand of law, ambled up to my door. I stared at them in mounting horror. I looked around frantically for moral support from the spouse, who being already dressed, was in a much stronger place confidence-wise than I could ever be in a faded tee and a pair of track pants that had emerged from the factory at approximately the same time that Michael Jackson was still a black boy.

'Kanan Mehra kone?' one of them asked. Me. That was my name.

I nodded meekly. 'Yes, I am Kanan. Mee Kanan aahe,' I replied in my stilted Marathi, careful to keep the shrill sound of panic out of my voice. 'Kay zhalay bhau?'

It occurred to me that this was perhaps not the best conversation to have at my doorstep. Especially since the live-in servant from the flat up front had opened his door and was staring at us with the unabashed curiosity of the unselfconscious. In fact, he had settled himself against the door to get a good unhindered view of the proceedings, rubbing his snuff into his palm, probably to set the right mood. My name would be mud in the society by the end of the day. I called shrilly for the lawfully betrothed to take charge of the situation. He emerged from the dark corner he'd hidden himself in, most probably the balcony where he sneaks off for a quick smoke, far from my searching, sharpened-with-wifely-concern eyes.

'What is the problem?' he asked, gesturing for the policemen to come inside.

'We are here on an investigation,' the swarthier of the two began. The other, thinner and more curious about the contents of my house than the former, judging by the neck-swivelling in process, nodded in support of what his colleague had just said and mopped his face with a handkerchief.

'We are here on a murder investigation,' the face-mopper said, tucking in his sweat-drenched handkerchief into a back pocket. My face turned a shade of sickly green more suitable for a corpse than a living being.

Kabir bounded up, hearing the word murder with his elephant ears that pick up anything remotely gruesome. 'Wherez d CID?' he demanded petulantly, his idea of cops being from the totally age-inappropriate serial he watches on television. The swarthy one cast an eye towards Kabir and cracked a smile that split his face into half like a melon, revealing an incredibly pink tongue behind gleaming white teeth.

'Come here, hero,' he called Kabir, who with the total lack of fear that comes from childhood innocence, marched right up to him and demanded to be shown his gun. The police inspector happily took out said weapon and displayed it to His Wide-Eyedness, who promptly went into his room and emerged with the exact same model. Albeit in plastic. And looked his most intimidating while aiming it at said cop.

Pleasantries dealt with, the policemen turned their attentions to me. 'Do you know this person?' Swarthy asked me, displaying a rather sad passport photograph of a woman I vaguely knew as a morning walker I smiled and nodded to every morning as we passed each other huffing and puffing on the back road route we took. In fact, I had seen her just that morning. We had never actually gotten around to exchanging names, or initiating what could be a conversation.

He pulled out a series of photographs of what seemed to be a lady lying on a road, with a scarily deep gash across her throat, which made my knees so weak, that had I been standing, I would have surely collapsed to the floor and broken a couple of tiles with the impact.

'She's dead?' I shrieked, quite horrified that I would have one less person to nod and smile at on my arms-bent, knees-straight, shoulders-back routine.

'Murrderr ho gaya,' said Cop 2, no longer sweating gallons. The spouse, quick to be hospitable, had switched the air-conditioning to an arctic blast. 'Sheetal Jaiswal. Lives in the E Wing of your complex.'

Cop 1 made a swift movement to indicate the throat being slit. 'Gala kaat diya,' he informed us. 'We are here to collect information for the panchnama.'

It had happened in the morning, they told me. She had lain, bleeding to death for over thirty minutes till the next morning walker had passed that way. The security guards and the driver/car-washer nexus had already been questioned, and according to the information gathered from them and other morning walkers, the police guessed that I had passed her approximately ten to fifteen minutes before she had been attacked. I was on my way back to the building complex and she was on her way out.

'Yes,' I croaked, before clearing my throat. 'I knew her. But I didn't *know* her, you know . . . I hadn't ever spoken with her.'

Cop 1 noticed the fear on my face and hastened to reassure me. 'Madam, don't take tension,' he said, cracking his face into a smile which could have scared a pregnant woman into labour. 'We are not suspecting you of murdering her,' he guffawed noisily as if the thought were too hilarious to digest, making me feel rather offended that I wasn't intimidating enough to be considered capable of murder.

'We know you passed her as she went out for her morning walk. We just needed the exact time.'

'I get back home at around 6.30 a.m. every day,' I replied. 'So I must have passed her around 6.15ish.'

And were there any other people on the road at that time whom I recognised or remembered, they asked.

I had passed a number of familiar faces from the complex, and named them all to him. Along with the flat and wing numbers, if I knew and remembered them.

The building complex we lived in was rather huge. Built on land reclaimed from the marshes, it sprawled out in an elongated U shape with the arms of the U cradling a patch of green below which doubled as children's park and joggers track where residents could congregate in the mornings and evenings for their daily constitutionals and dose of fresh air and gossip. Ten years ago, the swamps here were notorious as dumping grounds for murdered corpses. Today smooth roads and glass-fronted buildings announced what it had become—a business district. The residential complexes were a minuscule part of the entire project, constructed so that folk could live in close proximity to their work. We had moved in here barely a couple of years ago, along with around two hundred other families, and the complex was now a tropical ecosystem of its own.

My mind drifted to what had been bothering me ever since I'd been told about Sheetal being done in: how had I not got the buzz about a murder having been committed in the near vicinity through the entire day? With my trusted grapevine, I should have been in the loop the moment the body had been found. After all, wasn't I the acknowledged queen of the gossips in the complex?

Shame on me and my networking skills. I should find that spoonful of water and dunk myself into it head first. I made a mental note to call friend in building E and berate her soundly on not letting me know about such a monumental development happening in our sleepy, suburban apartment complex. Such laxity did not augur well for the women's network of information.

'What was she wearing?' Swarthy interrupted my thoughts. 'Do you remember?'

Sure, I replied confidently. She was wearing grey tracks and a faded pink T-shirt with Billabong written on the front; a pair of white Nike shoes, with pink stripes on the side; and she had her iPod ear plugs shoved deep into her auditory canal. Hadn't they just shown me gruesome pictures of her wearing exactly that?

They looked at each other, 'Are you sure?' asked Sweaty.

'Yes,' I replied confidently. Sheetal Jaiswal had three standard outfits which she had been rotating for the past two years. Pink, yellow and grey T-shirts with the same brand name emblazoned on the front, worn with grey, navy or pink track pants. She was not a woman who invested too much in exercise wear. They didn't elaborate on what it was about my description that had them look at each other in furrowed-brow concern.

Seeing a person every day for almost two years makes one notice little details even if he or she was not a thing of beauty and a joy forever. I mentioned hesitantly that she had her hair tied off her face into a scanty ponytail with a pale pink scrunchy, and plastered down to the scalp with the help of a grey, pink and white striped headband. Had to hand it to the recently deceased lady; she had been meticulous about coordinating her accessories.

Sweaty cleared his throat. Swarthy examined the pictures again with a beady eye. 'Actually, Madam, unke shoes kuch alag the. She was found wearing a pair of gents shoes.' He fished out a photograph where I could see clearly that the lady had in fact been wearing a pair of rather ugly shoes of indeterminate colour which were clearly manufactured in the factory for the male gender. Curiouser and curiouser. Why would a murderer divest her of her perfectly nice pair of running shoes and put on a pair of really fugly, scruffy shoes. And waste precious time doing so?

It didn't make sense. Not that many things made sense to me anyway. The biggest thing that didn't make sense to me was why someone would kill Sheetal Jaiswal. She'd seemed harmless enough; but of course I knew nothing about her, she wasn't one who socialised with the neighbours or with the others in the complex. In fact, the most one had interacted with her was when we stood around in patriotic bonhomie at the amphitheatre down in the park every Independence Day or Republic Day and sang the national anthem in assorted toneless voices.

I was ashamed to realise that she was someone I had not attempted to get to know. I hung my head at my lack of friendliness; I, who considered myself to be the metaphoric Golden Retriever of the complex, bounding up to new, confused residents, knocking them over and sniffing their crotches. Err. No. Keep that at bounding over and making friends indiscriminately, and occasionally biting someone in the thigh.

But I hadn't done more than smile politely at Sheetal Jaiswal. She wasn't the type that encouraged random conversation. She always seemed steeped in a layer of doom and gloom, with downturned lips set in a disgruntled face. Like she perennially had a bad smell under her nose.

She had been the same size since the time I had seen her begin her morning walks, a pleasantly rotund size, so I couldn't even put her death down to jealousy (given that I had often contemplated a well-aimed ice pick—inspired of course by Sharon Stone, panty-less, and in control in *Basic Instinct*—straight to the heart of one stick-thin model-type with absolutely zero body fat who ran down the same route I took every morning, wearing cycling shorts and tank tops that ensured that every male out for a morning constitutional got a crick in the neck as she passed them).

The little jewellery she was wearing had still been on her when she was found, the police informed us. Her earrings (two gold studs), and a thin bracelet. No rings. All that was missing was a thin gold chain and a pendant, which was a fake one, with a religious icon on it and not worth the gold plating it had on, according to these, the incredibly long arms of the law. And her iPod was found lying a few feet away from her body. All this pretty much did away with the murder-for-money theory. Unless, of course, the thin gold chain had caught the murderer's bloodshot eye and had tempted him to put knife to throat.

I wondered what kind of music she had been listening to when the murderer had crept up behind her and slashed her throat. That the murderer had indeed crept up from behind and slashed her throat was, of course, pure conjecture on my part. The cops had not said anything to me. This didn't stop me from imagining the scene though—and all I had to go on was the little I'd seen in movies and crime serials, of which *CID* forms an important component being a favourite with the child. Blood must have gurgled up, when the knife cut through the jugular. I felt queasy at the thought. I cannot, repeat cannot, stand the sight or smell of blood from a human or an animal source.

I actually passed out when the spouse first took me with him to buy the weekly supply of animal flesh. The sight of the goat's beady eye glaring at me from a head kept nonchalantly on a counter was enough for me to dovetail headfirst to the ground. And very mucky ground at that, it being the monsoon season. The spouse has since, sensibly, handled all meat-buying duties himself, with me stepping in only in a crunch, and only when said animal and avian flesh can be picked up cleaned, cut and packaged out of a freezer at the hypermarket.

Putting a known face to a slit throat made my insides heave, and I wondered if I could last the interview without barfing all over my spotless floor. To my credit, I did. I gulped nervously a few times, but held my bile.

The cops took down the details I supplied them with and took off. I breathed in relief as the policemen stood at the lifts, pressing the button impatiently, popping packets of pan masala into their mouths. Now that I was quite sure that I was not going to be led off, manacled, into solitary imprisonment with only rats the size of Pomeranian dogs for company in the jail cell and a hole in the ground for a toilet, and no access to my Blackberry or eyeliner, mirror and lipstick, I was fine.

The domestic help of the flat opposite was still perched in his position, seeming a trifle disappointed that none of the family was being led off handcuffed to the dungeons. He was already getting the lowdown of what had been discussed from my maid, in hushed tones which implied more sinister detail was being given than I cared for to be given. I called her in with a short, sharp bark. I didn't want the entire building to be looking at me like I was the murder suspect from the next day—although I could surely do with some particularly BO-challenged folk keeping their distance from me when in the close confines of the elevator.

The neighbour from the far end of the corridor ambled across. 'Kanaaaaan,' she said in elevated tones and eyebrows which expressed her concern. 'Whatever happened, why are the cops here?' Her brow was creased in a worried frown, a hastily pulled together wrap indicating a state of dishabille that denoted the day had almost ended for her.

Meena, for that's what her name was, was a TV actress. She had played roles in those television soaps that involved complicated multigenerational plots which had made her a household name. She could be accused of singlehandedly setting unrealistic expectations about daughters-in-law in the heads of every mother-in-law in the TV-watching universe. Her serial was now done with, and she was spending quite a lot of time—as she said to the press whenever asked—reading scripts and concept notes.

Evidently it was a hell of a lot of reading, and therefore she did not get much time to actually work. The truth of the matter was, the viewing public would need a substantial break before they would even accept her in another role—she'd become so strongly associated with the character she had played. Besides, she was tired of playing the dutiful bahu; after all, she had confessed to me once in a rare moment of candidness, how long could she keep giving the same martyred expression in close-ups taken from different angles. The good thing was, she *could* still convey expressions in this era of Botox-frozen faces. Meena, thankfully, kept her face unfrozen. It was very helpful during such animated conversations.

'A lady from the E Wing has been murdered,' I hissed. 'This morning.' Unmindful of the child standing gape-mouthed between both of us, already draped in an old discarded jacket of mine, and a Goa flea market hat, and holding a magnifying glass in readiness to play detective, influenced, no doubt, by the Nate the Great book series which were a current obsession.

'I am looking for clues,' he announced to no one in particular and began tracking some invisible footprints down the corridor.

We ignored him, as adults discussing something earth-shattering that normally involves an extramarital affair, stunning weight loss by a friend of a common acquaintance or, as in this case, the murder of someone we had a passing acquaintance with.

We discussed intensely the lack of safety for morning walkers (not that Meena was one), and the fear of not being able to step out unguarded. And we debated furiously about whether dead people come back as ghosts to haunt the spot they were murdered to take their revenge. Ghosts would be off duty during daylight hours, we concluded, so it would probably be safe for us to go on our walks after sunrise. But just to be safe, would it be better to get a havan done there to rid the area of said potential spirits of murdered women?

It was terrible, the thought that it could have been any one of us out there, with our throats slit from end to end, feeling the blood and the life ebb out of us as we lay sprawled in an undignified way on the asphalt. With men's shoes on our feet and a gold chain torn off our neck, a chain taken off before or after the neck was cut, one wondered. And we shuddered collectively at the thought.

Our conversation was interrupted by a discreet bellow from the spouse. I hurried back before steam began emanating from his nostrils. He was one minute away from pawing the ground with his hooves, err, shoes. There was a party to attend. Yes, the red paint on the nails had dried up. And yes, it was a little smudged. But then, what was some smudged nail paint when terribly exciting things like murder were part of the evening?

# CHAPTER 3

# IN WHICH MUCH GAPING AT A BOLLYWOOD SUPERSTAR HAPPENS

**W**HEN WE ENTERED, the party was just about heating up. Read, we were early. Very early. And we were one entire hour past the start time mentioned on the invite. In elegant cursive font. Printed on onion paper in gold. In a manner so elegant, I thought it was a wedding invite.

In fact, we were so early, that the waiters looked at us quizzically, and there seemed to be no one else apart from the event management team standing around with little pieces of something stuck into their ears, speaking in hushed tones to themselves and rushing around looking Very Busy and Not Likely To Appreciate Being Asked When The Party Would Start.

I threw the spouse the I Told You So look. This was a look that was pursuant to the vociferous discussion we'd had in the car about it being okay if we were an hour late for a party, because no party worth its guest list starts on time. And given that we received a printed invitation card, with our names typewritten on them (with the husband's first name spelt wrong, you can't hit a man lower than spelling his name wrong!), it wasn't as if we could hope that this was going to be an intimate exclusive insider do.

The husband is a stickler for punctuality, which is of course a wonderful quality when it comes to catching flights and attending meetings and such like, but he therefore doesn't understand that you cannot, just cannot, reach a party on the time printed on the invite. It is a faux pas beyond faux pas. It is the uncrowned king of bad etiquette. It shows you have nothing better to do with your time than ensure you are on time. It is something even us moms master when we have to escort the little ones to birthday parties. Reaching on time puts you on the bottom of the evolutionary ladder, and automatically marks you out as a wannabe.

The spouse does not have much experience attending parties. All the partying he's done was in his early youth when college and the promise of women and alcohol had lured him to college socials. After he got into management school and emerged pruned to management speak and spreadsheets and a career that hinged on him spending as much time at office as was humanly possible without physically shifting into the premises with suitcases and a toothbrush, his partying days had all but come to a standstill. Now his idea of a night out was a trip to the sports bar to watch the finals of some mega sporting event and drown enough gallons of beer to flood a urinal.

So he has no idea that even for a party that has balloons, cartoon characters and a cake as its main attractions, one must reach at least an hour late. And for a party that will have film stars, alcohol and Page 3-ites, you need to pour yourself into the room at an hour you think the rest of the crowd are pouring themselves out, even if it means circling the block ten times, and then calling and checking with the unlucky sods already in about attendance levels and, of course, whether the bar is open.

The only other person looking as puzzled as the spouse was a man, dressed oddly enough—even though it was the so-called winter in Mumbai—in a black velvet smoking jacket over a V-necked tee and scruffy jeans, and pointed cowboy shoes. His hair, which partly obscured his face, was a mass of unruly curls, and he seemed taller than average. He looked confused. Whether it was unfamiliarity with the limited number of guests present, or a general state of confusedness, I could not tell.

I stared at him, trying to figure out whether he was stare-able because he was a promising newcomer on the Bollywood circuit or someone famous I should know, or simply because he was so very stare-able. I concluded that the last held true. But as a respectably married woman, it was unseemly to stare at a man, especially when the husband was growling at one's arm, therefore I contented myself by pointing him out to the spouse and saying, 'There, one more early bird. Do you know him?'

'No,' said the spouse in his usual tone that brooked no further discussion, as he looked for the furthest corner in which to bury himself so he wouldn't be compelled to mingle and conduct animated conversation with pleasant folks who attended parties to do just that. For such an anti-social person, it was a miracle he had managed to survive in a field like marketing for so very long without being scooted out on his very pinchable butt. I scurried behind him just as the clock at the far end of the banquet hall struck nine.

The room was slowly beginning to fill up with variants of the lowest algae from the social stratosphere. The starlets, the hangers-on, the folk with no real profession to speak of, except that of party-attendees. They flocked into the venue in groups, chattering away and air-kissing as they spotted each other. Some glued to texting or twittering on their mobiles.

Remember that adage about eating healthy before you go for a party to ensure that you don't end up overeating unhealthy fried stuff that does really bad things to your arteries and cholesterol levels and ends up as heart sludge guaranteed to knock you off to an early grave? I don't. And my stomach was making unseemly growling sounds which could have fooled a tropical jungle of animals into believing a lion was close at hand. So I sat in the way of every random waiter who passed with a tray of starters, even hailing down a few who strayed off the path, and popped each happily into my mouth.

The husband waited with a face growing increasingly dark for the person who had invited him, so he could show face, mark his attendance at the event and vamoose. The lure of free alcohol at a do might tempt a lesser man to stay on longer than required, but not the spouse. If the spouse had his way, he would heli-drop himself on a desert island with only his laptop and wireless broadband connection for company (after having ensured some way to charge the battery of said laptop of course, perhaps through solar panel generators) and live happily ever after fishing for his lunch, and watching the sun set over the ocean, guzzling his beer (having also ensured a lifetime supply of beer to said desert island).

The spouse kept himself busy by messaging frenetically. If I could take a hammer to the Blackberry in his hand, I would. Sometime. I was convinced his thumb moved on its own accord even when he was deep in REM sleep.

I looked around at the crowd and noticed that Velvet Smoking Jacket had now perched himself at the bar right at the distant end of the room, having found company in a girl so luscious that her strapless dress was staying upright only through willpower or strategically applied two-way tape. I noticed with interest that the Velvet Smoking Jacket was looking into her eyes and having a conversation. A difficult task given the spillage that was happening right under his chin.

Some excited squeals announced the arrival of Baby Doll. Born a man in Allahabad, and made a woman in Bangkok, she simpered in with a spaghetti-strap dress that showed off her recently acquired cleavage to such advantage that had her push-up bra been any tighter strapped, her chin would have been buried in her chest. She was fiercely clutching on to the arm of a strapping young fellow who seemed somewhat embarrassed to be the one being held, but looked like he was here to be her official arm candy.

The next to arrive were the models. Some of them with eyes so dilated that they didn't seem to register what was around them—just jumped straight onto the dance floor, or disappeared into dark corners where undoubtedly credit cards were being put to very good use. And not for shopping, if you know what I mean.

The spouse finally spotted the man who had invited us and jumped to his feet to congratulate the chappie just as a sudden hush descended on the entire room and all eyes moved in a sort of weird synchronicity towards the door. The room, if it could stand up, was standing up.

At the door, looking undecided and amazingly fresh-faced, was the bad boy superstar of Bollywood, Suhaan Khan, surrounded by an entourage of what seemed like bodyguards, assorted relatives and friends and some random press folks, distinguished by the fact that they didn't look dressed for the event, and yet didn't seem like they felt out of place.

The spouse's hand was pumped hastily and distractedly by friend. People turned back to what they were doing before Suhaan Khan had made an appearance, though it seemed like everyone kept one eye darting around to check up on whom he was speaking with and which part of the room he was meandering through.

I sat back on my just vacated seat, having sprung from it in true village hick manner when I realised I was in the presence of a Bollywood superstar. I now realised I was in direct line of sight of the table Suhaan Khan had chosen and tugged the husband's trousers for his attention, which was being devoted exclusively to his Scotch neat.

I muttered while keeping my mouth appropriately agape, a tough task if you ever care to try it, 'That's Suhaan Khan.'

I got the look which stated 'Do Not Behave Like A Hillbilly and Ruin My Reputation aka Do Not Go Squawking Across For An Autograph'. The look didn't register. So words were used to get the message across. 'Don't even think of going across for an autograph,' the love of my life muttered through clenched teeth. 'Come on,' he said, helping me to my feet. I thought he'd had a swift change of mind and decided to help me get an autograph, so I fished around in my copper-beaded clutch for a scrap of paper and a pen. My knees were trembly at the thought of meeting Suhaan Khan. I prayed they wouldn't give way, and I wouldn't fall down in a melodramatic manner just as I reached his table. *Or*, maybe he would help me up and wonder where I had been all his life?

The spouse glared at me with eyes that could slice butter. Frozen butter. 'Put that paper back,' he hissed. 'We're leaving now. This party is becoming too filmy.'

What? Wasn't it a filmy party to begin with? Where had I got the memo wrong?

'No,' I squawked in protest. 'I'm sitting right here. Let's wait a while.' The alcohol I'd imbibed fortified me to defy spousal authority with a calm and equanimity I did not normally have in abundant reserve.

At that precise moment Suhaan turned around and cast a cursory glance around the premises; his eyes passed over me. I imagined he winked. Or his eyes twinkled. They definitely twinkled, if it was not a wink. Wild horses couldn't drag me from the spot now.

I sat down with a resoluteness that would do any person sitting down for a dharna proud. The chair creaked in protest.

'I don't want to go home now,' I stated as firmly as I could and plucked a corn kabab off the tray of a waiter floating around. 'Eat something,' I urged the spouse grandly, with the kind of largesse that comes from being at someone else's party and not worrying about whether supplies will run out.

He shook his head. The spouse has immense self-control when it comes to food intake. I balance the two of us out. Which is why I have cellulite and he doesn't.

'I'm getting myself a drink, do you want anything?' he asked resignedly, knowing that once I have settled for the evening, only the close of the party and guests being physically thrown out will get my rump to raise itself from its seat.

I nodded and said, 'The usual.'

He disappeared into the throng of folks battling to get the harried bartender's attention, like a good spouse should, to keep his woman hydrated and happy.

'So,' said a deep, crisp, unfamiliar voice at my elbow, 'is this the first time you're seeing him in person?'

I jumped up in fright, not used to being spoken to randomly by folk I don't know. It was the Velvet Smoking Jacket. His voice was appropriately velvety. His eyes were fringed with shamefully feminine lashes. Or was it mascara? I squinted to check. He looked awfully familiar in that vague way in which someone you think you should know but do not know is. I am slowly going into early Alzheimer's, I know. And yes, it was a trifle embarrassing to make a public admission to a strange Velvet Smoking Jacket that one was indeed a hillbilly who had never shared the air of a single room with a superstar.

'Is it that obvious?' I asked, wishing the earth would do another of those Mother Earth Swallow Me Now and Belch Me Up Later moments, without of course primordial goo clinging to my copper-flecked top.

'Yes, it is,' he said bluntly, adding a smile to soften said bluntness. 'Enjoy yourself,' he added laconically and moved on to some distant periphery of the room, no doubt to consort with women with more finesse than to stare open-mouthed at superstars who were now looking around with an air of aggrieved boredom.

I swallowed hard and firmly, and I thought efficiently, and distracted myself by examining the other people populating the room. I saw some minor female film stars walk in, accompanied by their dress designers and film producers who are safe escorts because no one would ever link them, given producers usually have an orientation towards the male of the species. These were the beautiful people of our film industry and a lot of time and effort had been spent in making them beautiful.

They gravitated to Suhaan Khan, and the lackeys made place at the table for them. Suhaan Khan had recently split up from his long-time and very young girlfriend, and was therefore in the market for company. According to the gossip vine, he had always been in the market for company.

The spouse returned, bearing a Scotch for himself and a Screwdriver for me. I took it gratefully, and downed it in a couple of unladylike gulps, comfortable in the knowledge that enough food had made its way into my intestines to steady the absorption of the alcohol, and ensure I didn't get onto a table top and start belting out an '80s hit.

Speaking of which, the DJ suddenly (albeit belatedly), got the message that it would be a good idea to play dance hits from Suhaan Khan's movies and the crowd roared its approval, the implicit request being that the man himself would get up and shake a leg or two to the songs being played.

It was obvious the man was loath to do so. He looked lazily around at the expectant faces around him. His eyes settled on mine and he half smiled. Had I been a teenager, I would have squealed and fainted. And squealed and fainted once again. But I was older, more mature and therefore I just squealed. One single squeal that was happily lost in the noise.

The spouse did not notice, fortunately, because he had found one sole person he knew and had latched onto him expediently, and was happily imparting gyaan about something said person was least interested in knowing. The spouse's conversation, lovely person that he is, does not veer very far from what he is comfortable with—the stock market, the political situation in Maoist India and the

Indian economy. And he has the wonderful skill of turning every conversation right back to what his realm of expertise is, even if the person he is speaking with has a glaze in his eyes, and is going into anaphylactic shock.

Suhaan Khan was now playing the superstar to the hilt, surveying the room and paying no attention to the two nubile hopefuls perched at his table. His bodyguards swept the room with gazes that were as serrated as chainsaws. After five minutes, the superstar lazily picked himself up and sauntered off, leaving the women and quite a few men looking after him, like tugboats in the wake of a steam ship. His entourage picked themselves off the assorted furniture they had draped themselves on, and the hosts ran to bow and scrape on his entire route to the exit. Five minutes later, the spouse decided it was the right time for us to exit too, and as I had lost all interest in the party, now that my close encounter with celebrity was done, I agreed.

As I passed the bar on my way out, I spotted Velvet Smoking Jacket now sitting with a streaked-hair, mini-skirted glamazon. He saw me, raised his glass, and gave me a quick wink. It hit me like a sudden pinch on the butt would. You must realise, I do not get winked at often. Oh well, let's be realistic, I do not get winked at at all these days. My days of being winked at have long passed. I lowered my head and marched out, sure that the entire world and its bouncers could see my cheeks flaming red, and not from the Screwdriver or the sweeping strokes of the Bronze Shimmer Brick I'd slathered on with a more forceful hand than usual.

The spouse was striding out ahead of me. 'Wait for me,' I squeaked angrily, and minced behind him on my too-high strappy stilettos.

# CHAPTER 4

# IN WHICH THERE IS YET ANOTHER CORPSE

**O**N THE WAY BACK HOME, the roads were not deserted. In fact, Friday night partying was still in full swing, enough to make the rush on the roads seem like we were en route to an IPL final. Or semi-final. Or anything that would have the entire city out on the streets. Which included free ice cream being distributed at every signal. But alas, that was not to be. I was pleasantly tipsy enough to suggest that the evening could still be continued. Alcohol does that to me; it puts me in a realm beyond all rationality.

'Why don't we go somewhere?' I asked, the alcohol causing a pleasant buzz in my ears, which it does when it has been combined with enough deep-fried and cholesterol-causing starters. I could feel the fat cells yippee in glee as they found new friends and comrades to swell their ranks. I could feel the thighs popping and skin stretching to accommodate the new entrants.

'Where?' asked the spouse in his typical monosyllabic manner which was meant to discourage further discussion on the topic.

I was buzzed enough to ignore the faint warning in his voice though. 'Let's go to a club . . .' He raised a warning eyebrow. The spouse was of the old school of thought that believed clubbing was an activity reserved for those with their hearing intact, and their sleep needs still at a point where they could function normally the subsequent day with minimal REM. He, on the other hand, required eight hours of deep undisturbed sleep to feel human the subsequent day.

'Listen,' he began, the No in his voice loud and clear before it actually tripped off his tongue, 'I might have to go into work tomorrow. And I can't sleep in the afternoon like you.'

I turned to face the window and sulked at the implication that the most important thing in my entire day was my afternoon nap. (Though, honestly speaking, it is. Only the very brave and those with a death wish dare to wake me up from an afternoon nap. Those who have lived to tell the tale have had chewed-off ears as evidence of their bravery/stupidity.) I bristled enough to have my quills up on edge, and pouted at the window. Settling myself into my seat, I tweeted furiously about being in touching distance of Suhaan Khan at the party and got many jealous tweets in response from Suhaan Khan-fan types on my timeline.

Suddenly, the car screeched to a hitting-head-against-dashboard halt. No, I hadn't got my seat belt on. I never do. It constricts me. Yes, I know, I deserve to be thrown out of the windscreen and sustain fatal cranial injuries. But it seemed, looking at the crumpled heap on the road in front of us, that someone had already received fatal cranial injuries.

'Shit, shit, shit,' the spouse swore. He reserves his actual son-of-the-soil swearing for his casual conversations with his friends. The rest of the time, he is purged and clean of actual offensive language. 'Looks like a hit-and-run.'

We carefully got out of the car to check. I tottered over as quick as them five-inchers allowed me and stood horrified next to the spouse as we gazed down at a man who very clearly had no life in him. And the hole bang in the centre of the forehead indicated that it was probably not a hit-and-run. The spouse anyway kneeled and checked the man's pulse, just in case. Nada, he gestured. Not a beep. He looked up and down the deserted back road we had taken in a bid to skip traffic signals, at an hour when traffic signals were automatically switched off. Now we knew why back roads remained deserted, while the main roads choked with traffic. His look was furtively guilty, like he was the one who had taken aim at said centre of forehead from sixty paces.

'What now? Shall we take him to a hospital, or shall we call the cops?' he asked, looking genuinely perplexed. Dealing with random corpses found lying in the middle of a road close to midnight was in no management training manual. My intestines were heaving, and I was in no situation to provide a coherent answer.

What *was* the protocol when one discovered a corpse of what seemed like a relatively hale and hearty thirty-something male, approximately five foot ten inches, wearing what seemed like drainpipe trousers, those pointed leather shoes that always made me go Uggh, and a purple satin shirt. The face was obscured by all the blood that had trickled down it, like the rivulets to an estuary, from the rather unsightly hole in his forehead. The fringe of the tiny hole was slightly blackened, as though burnt.

'Call the police,' I shrieked at the husband, holding onto the bonnet of the car for support. 'This is a dead man here.' I reviewed the situation, and repeated in shrill tones, 'This is a murdered man.'

A chilly finger climbed its way up my spine, in the manner that chilly fingers of ether do when one confronts creatures from the other world. Two corpses in one day were a bit too much for a kind, gentle soul like me to handle. I could feel the bile rising to my throat. I turned around quickly and spattered the edge of the paved road with all the starters I had consumed gleefully barely an hour ago, taking care to ensure there was no splashing on my fake LV shoes. The spouse handed his handkerchief so I could wipe my mouth. I did the needful and handed said handkerchief back, which he discarded in disgust.

He dialled a number on his cell phone and spoke to a disembodied voice. 'Yes, dead body. On the road behind Primavarus Mall. Male.' He paused. 'Yes, I'm sure. He's totally dead.'

The voice barked something indistinct. 'Of course I know he's dead. He's not breathing.'

More disembodied commands.

Further pause. 'Okay, we are waiting here.' Another long drawn-out pause. 'No, of course I didn't kill him. Why would I call you if I had?'

He hung up and told me, 'That's the local police inspector who came over this evening. I'd saved his number. Just in case.' The spouse always has numbers he's saved 'just in case'. This habit has saved our skin one zillion times. I nodded glumly, wishing I had an anti-emetic to keep the contents of my stomach down. That was the last time I was eating lots of fried stuff before coming across dead bodies, I told myself.

And so we waited. We stood by the bonnet of the car and stared at the body. It is strange looking at a corpse that had no connection with you while the body was still alive. You start to dissect it, dispassionately wondering who the person was and how he came about to be dead. The clothes were of the kind worn by them stretched-grin types who dance behind the lead actor in a Bollywood song. Or the kind worn by men who love other men. Or the kind worn by a person attending a party where the theme is retro and shiny satiny shirts in purple are the height of chic.

Standing on my five-inch heels was making my calves cramp, and I moved back into the car to sit comfortably. The world, thankfully, wasn't spinning anymore. And now that I was firmly planted on a solid surface, I could think clearly too.

Would the police bring along the press? Would there be television cameras from assorted news channels checking out the corpse? I thanked the lord for the invention of wet wipes and quickly used one to remove the last traces of bile from my lips. One must always be prepared for one's possible five minutes of fame, so I dug out my compact and powdered myself to perfection in the dim car light, fixing eyeliner that had wandered off to where it had no business travelling without permission, and slapping on a layer of additional lip gloss for maximum wet-look drool-worthiness. If there was half a chance I was going to be on television, I had to at least get the look right. What would I say? Did I have time to prepare an agonised expression; or should I behave all cool and soignée, like almost driving over corpses was part of a day's work for me?

And then it struck me, we were two minutes away from home. In fact, we were right at the exact spot where Sheetal Jaiswal had been found with her throat slit open that very morning. Two corpses in a day at the same spot were a bit too much for delicate nerves like mine.

I am not a brave woman. I screech when panicked, and I panic easily. People lock me away in situations that require a cool head and calm handling. I can be counted on to create even more of a mess than already exists. I am also kept away at marriage negotiations. I shuddered, imagining a serial killer, wild-eyed and manic, hidden behind the shrubs skirting the road. Gooseflesh bumped my arms.

Luckily, the sound of the siren from an oncoming police jeep didn't give me any more time to think. It screeched to a halt inches away from us, and four men emerged, including two policemen in khaki, looking weary and a little disgruntled that their peaceful night watch had been disturbed for this, of all things. A random dead body.

'Ithe, ithe,' one cop yelled to the other who was looking around at the scenery. 'Dead body ithe ahe.'

Another man, a camera hung around his neck, got to quick work clicking photographs of the corpse and the road around said corpse from different angles. The police inspector scratched his rotund belly absently and stared at the body for a good five minutes before turning his attention to us. Another cop in civil clothes scanned the road with a flashlight.

He lapsed into Hindi with us. 'What time did you drive by?'

'Around 11.30 p.m.,' said the spouse without missing a beat. He was pretty cool, this man I'd married. He could deal with cops without quivering in his shoes, or getting knock-kneed and sweaty-palmed like I did, even without committing the crime. I, unfortunately, look guilty if a person in authority so much as passes a stray eye over me if I am standing in a crowd. Even if I don't even know what crime has been committed. If I did get picked out of the crowd, I would probably confess to the crime in question, convinced the detectives were going to take me into a backroom and beat me to a pulp to extract a confession out of me.

Just then, an ambulance joined our little gang, ostensibly to remove the body to a morgue and to the undignified post-mortem that no doubt awaited it.

A crew of white uniformed ward boy types hopped off the ambulance, bearing a stretcher between them, and loaded the purple-shirted body into the ambulance with the kind of apathy that comes from dealing with corpses on a daily basis. A grim-faced tiny man in police uniform was circling the spot making notes in a small notepad.

'Okay,' the belly-scratcher was taking down names and asking for identification. 'Didn't your missus get a visit this evening from two sub-inspectors from our station enquiring about the Sheetal Jaiswal murder?'

He fixed a couple of beady eyes on me and I shrank further and further into the foliage that fringed the road, hoping that disappearing behind the spouse would render me invisible. Unfortunately, surely a lot of me was visible even with the spouse standing bang in front of me. Someday, these hips are going to get me stuck in a revolving door. Anyway. Coming back to the cop eyeing me suspiciously. The spouse shifted in a sweet attempt to shield me from the policeman's gaze. 'Yes,' he answered tersely, with the implied, 'So what are you trying to say?' writ loud and clear enough for even a seasoned tough nut cop to quail. Did it really seem like I was the prime suspect, being connected to every murder at this location? Was everything really about me?

And then, from the distance, I heard the screeching of the TV news vans I'd powdered myself up for, but now I didn't feel like I needed the attention. I was sure my nose was shiny with the cold sweat I'd broken out into.

CHAPTER 5

# IN WHICH THERE IS A TYPICAL SUBURBAN WEEKEND

**I**T WAS NOT A NICE, relaxed Saturday. The husband decided he was too overwrought with the events of the previous evening to attend office half-day as is his norm, even when not required to do so.

All of Saturday, the news channels went gaga over the presumed serial killer terrorising the residents of our neighbourhood. I learned from the channels that we were too scared to step out of our homes, and our children hadn't attended school. The fact that it was a weekend and, ergo, there was no school, was apparently incidental.

The intercom had been buzzing off its cradle all through the night, from the time I sent out my first sms to my current best friend in the whole world, Raji, who lived in the same building as me, about having discovered another dead body at approximately the same moment that the police van zoomed off with the corpse. Everyone from Mrs Kapur, the white-haired matron with her matching white Pomeranian, to each individual member of the gang of girls wanted the gruesome details. I repeated them ad infinitum. I embellished some minor details. And then further embellished them to such a degree that the body I had encountered and the body I described could have belonged to two separate dead people.

In the morning, Raji dropped in to extract every smidgeon of dead body gyaan from me in such inquisitor-like fashion I felt I could ace an interview for an assistant at a mortuary if required. After every nugget of information I gave her, she sighed with an air of distress, and then declared—after two rounds of kadak adrak wali chai strong enough to create a pleasant warmth down the throat that can only be rivalled by the finest cognac—that she was off to inspect the spot, and did I want to trot along with her to have a look-see in the light of day. I declined the offer politely. I had had quite enough of staring at the spot last night, and I described kindly for her the shape of the blood stain she would encounter which indicated where the head of said dead person had lain. The said dead person now had a name and an identity, Rohit Sharma, as I learnt from the newspapers.

A photograph of our building complex stared at me from Page 5 of India's Leading Newspaper, with a balcony circled. In red, no less. Sheetal Jaiswal's passport-sized face looked at me quizzically from further down in the article. Page 1 had already told us that our area had seen two gruesome murders in one day. And had a photograph of the man in the purple shirt, but dressed more sombrely this time, as befits a dead person. I realised he was quite good-looking without that blood running down his face. Rohit Sharma, they told us, in tones that brooked no argument, was an 'aspiring actor' having recently moved to Mumbai from a mofussil city up north, and presently put up at that Mecca of all Bollywood aspirants, namely

Lokhandwala in Andheri. The post-mortem results were yet to come, they said, but a source had revealed that the police were quite confident death had been caused by the bullet to the centre of the forehead. I concluded a bullet to the centre of the forehead would definitely cause death in any person. Unless of course, the person was already dead and said bullet had been delivered to make sure no revival was possible.

And there was the front pager two-column report on Sheetal Jaiswal. I learned more about her from the article than I had in the two years we'd been living in the same complex. She was thirty-eight years old, married to Manik Jaiswal. They had no children. She was found dead on the road at around 7 a.m. by a jogger who was passing by. There was no one to be seen on the road when he spotted her. The body had been taken for post-mortem where it showed that cause of death was blood loss from a deep cut to the throat. The motive behind the murder had not yet been established, but, according to initial speculation, this had been a simple case of robbery given that her neck had an abrasion where her gold chain seemed to have been pulled off. It was a thin gold chain with a Mata Vaishnodevi pendant, the article quoted the bereaved Mr Jaiswal as saying. There were, strangely, no pictures of the bereaved Mr Jaiswal, nor of any relatives bunched together with grim faces. Nor any mention absolutely of the strange shoes the lady was found wearing in lieu of her own. There was also, to my utter surprise, a quote from a 'neighbour', who said that Sheetal Jaiswal was a friendly woman, and had no enemies. I wondered which neighbour had been generous with his or her time and words to the media and why I had not been asked about my impressions about the recently deceased, having been technically the last person to have seen the recently deceased before she became the recently deceased.

'Look,' I showed the newspaper to the spouse who was shovelling down scrambled eggs on toast in the inelegant way a man does when he is truly hungry. 'This article about the murdered lady even has a photograph of our building complex.' The man moaned softly, muttering what vaguely sounded like self-censored epithets under his breath. The valuation of this property was definitely going to get impacted. And not for the better.

The phone rang, it was Mira on the line, Mira Gulati, my best friend from when we were knee-high and in pigtails back when mothers were responsible for our coiffeur and doused the fledgling tresses with half a bottle of coconut oil before we were considered respectable enough to make a public appearance. Mira now had plighted her troth to an investment banker type and lived in a condo with a private pool, with her daughter, hubby and omnipresent nanny.

'What's this, Kay?' she began without preamble and in a very accusatory tone, like I was personally responsible for dead people turning up in the neighbourhood, and guilty of keeping insider news from her. Mira takes unnatural deaths very seriously. She spends an allotted part of her mornings scanning the obituaries to check if anyone she knows personally has made it there, and then, if she manages to chance on a familiar name, spends the next allotted part of said morning calling up all and sundry to spread the gloom.

'Did you read the newspapers today? Have you switched on the news? There are people dying around your building complex.'

Errm. I had forgotten, in the rush of being the local celebrity, to inform my very best friend about my sudden elevation to prime witness in two murder cases. Mira sniffed out my sudden defensive demeanour without me saying a word. We two, the backbenchers at the strict convent school where rulers on the knuckles were accepted norm of correction and instruction, and of the delirious readings and re-readings of the kissing passages, helpfully flagged, in Mills & Boon books we borrowed from the local book library and smuggled into class, feeling much like voyagers on the Starship Enterprise, going where no sixth-grader in the class had gone before. 'Actually, Mira, hubby and I found the dead body of the chappie, and the lady who was killed on the road, I was I think the last person who saw her alive.'

'Whew!' she whistled. 'Kay Mehra, you do live!'

'Not exactly the best way to live, Mira, finding corpses all around and having cops beat down one's doors to get statements from you.'

'Tell me all,' she commanded, and I could just see her settling down on her raw silk upholstered chaise longue which was her preferred spot while having long, extended conversations with dearly beloved childhood friends like me. I settled myself into a similar comfortable spot with appropriate back rest and vantage point of both the kitchen and the kid's room before continuing, keeping both eyes swivelling in their sockets to ensure that nothing was crashing or burning, depending on the room in question.

'The cops actually came home to question you about Sheetal Jaiswal?' she squeaked. 'How exciting is that?' Mira is easily excitable. At her most excited she could be having a conversation with rodents.

I affirmed that I had, indeed, been granted a personal interview at my residence by the very long arms of our law and it had been a pleasant experience—no instruments of torture had been involved. 'How cool is that?' she squealed. 'Tell me, what does a dead body, with a gun shot to the head, actually look like?'

This was the moment I regretted not keeping my head about me and clicking quick pictures on the phone to show the infinite people who wanted descriptions of male corpse instead of doing totally unproductive things like barfing.

Mira always had this gruesome streak in her. She was the one who was quick with the frog dissections in biology, while I held my bile back and made throwing-up sounds much to the disgust of Sister Theresa who would tell me, with great distaste, to go sit on the bench outside the laboratory and compose myself or to keep my stomach empty before dissection.

We discussed murders, corpses, dieticians and seventy per cent sales at Mango, before deciding to meet up for lunch some fine day mid-week, and Mira gave me some sound advice which I tucked away at the back of my mind. 'Call Runa. She would love to stick her hands into this.'

Runa, being Runa Bhattarcharjee, one of ye olde gang from school days who currently eked out a living being a private investigator, spending most of her time taking on paid jobs like shadowing errant husbands and bored wives having a fling on the side, collecting photographic and other evidence which could swing things in her client's favour during divorce proceedings.

I promised her I would. Like most promises I make, I forget it promptly, with the pater calling immediately after I disconnected the call with Mira, and making me swear on all that was holy that I would not step out on deserted roads at odd times, and the mater insisting that I not step out at all, but just order in everything I needed, until the killers were caught and placed safely behind bars where they couldn't get to her daughter and grandson.

'Kay beta,' the concerned grandma stated, adding her two bits of advice, 'don't talk about dying and murder in front of the child. Such young children are very sensitive, it might impact him negatively.'

'Ah, Mamma, he watches *CID*. He knows more about murders than I do,' I replied in exasperation, thinking of a good way to end the conversation given that I would definitely be hauled over the coals for not monitoring the television-viewing habits of my only son, and ergo their only grandson, and the flag-bearer of their genetic inheritance given my brother was showing no signs of tying the official knot with a good Indian girl from a cultured family. Culture to the parents meant that the girl would know her wine glass from her water glass, and know how to work her cutlery from the outside in, if they were ever invited to dinner to any of their social circle.

Thankfully, the intercom rang. Insistently. 'Got to go, Ma. The intercom's buzzing.' She grumbled fussily about children these days having no time for a civil conversation with their parents who gave birth to them and raised them unselfishly. I took the opportunity to gently disconnect the call.

The parents, ex-civil servant and school teacher respectively, now living a retired life, pottering in their semi-detached bungalow on the outskirts of Pune, spent their mornings scanning the crime pages of the dailies and twice weekly evenings skyping with their only begotten son, and my younger brother, who was now playing at being a Very Eligible Hot Shot Bachelor In Software, based in London, firmly resisting all the photographs of suitable matrimonial candidates being emailed across the seas. The parents, filtering out the spawn of my womb, stayed in the vain hope that the only begotten son would settle down like softly-stirred tea leaves to a life of blissful matrimony and provide them with a much-longed-for grandchild to bear aloft the banner of their surname (they were not particular about gender of said future grandchild they specified carefully, in these politically correct times) before they closed their eyes and were consigned to the electric crematorium.

My parents were also practical. And thrifty. I grew up seeing my mother rinse out milk packets and sell them to the raddiwallah at the end of the month. We had gift-wrapping paper put underneath mattresses for reuse. The mater had a fetish for plastic bags and got into scraps at stores that refused her individual plastic bags for each item purchased. Her plastic bag collection was off limits to ordinary mortals, and if one needed a plastic bag in her home, one had to ask on bended knee, after which the worst of the lot would be grudgingly handed over. If I ever went into therapy, I think the recycled milk packets and the wrapping paper would play a starring role in my road to shopaholism and the pile of maxed-out credit card bills which had led to my being handed a debit card with a fixed limit by Cruel Spouse and the rest of the add-on cards being carefully snipped into tiny pieces and binned with the kind of sadistic glee that Hannibal Lecter might have reserved for his census taker.

The cops Sweaty and Swarthy were on the local cable channels, talking about their findings in the Sheetal Jaiswal murder case, which we realised as we watched was approximately zilch. The husband continued to moan and groan through the day about the depreciation in the property prices in the area, which would automatically depreciate the value of the house. I moaned and groaned about having to skip my morning walks, given an axe murderer had made venturing into the quiet back roads a bit of a death wish.

I gathered up the nerve to step down in the evening, occasioned by the child demanding to go down to the slides. The entire complex was in a lather. If one could imagine multi-storeyed towers grouped together around a token green park with jogging track and kid's play area being in a lather.

Hushed conversations at stairwells and in lobbies, and curious glances at strangers loitering around near the gates indicated that paranoia had set in. All the neighbourhood Lotharios who populated the road outside the gate waiting for the objects of their affections to emerge on their way to college/school/work were not-so-subtly encouraged to leave the area by security men.

Mrs Kapur, from the sixth floor of our building, declared that she was not going to skip her daily evening constitutional for some random axe murderer roaming the streets, but insisted she be accompanied by a watchman to ensure her safety. This led to a screaming match in the building lobby between the security rounder and Mrs Kapur, accentuated by Mrs Kapur's equally-white-haired Pomeranian, who took it upon herself to enliven the proceedings by nipping at the security rounder's ankles.

The issue was resolved by convincing Mrs Kapur that, if she chose to walk outside the complex, she was well protected by her dog: the yapping of the infernal creature would suffice to send Beelzebub right back to his furnace. And if her choice of location was within the complex, the security personnel would always be alert and active to deter the evil intentions of any blood-crazed psychopath who happened to scale the walls in search of fresh fodder for his knife.

'Arrey Madamji,' said Mr Rathore, Head Security Rounder, he of the marked resemblance to a large rodent, 'with us around, what do you need to fear?' An exhortation that Mrs Kapur took to heart and set off down the road promising to just go a little distance 'to the back road' and return promptly.

And of course, the rounder, who must always have the last word, especially when he is being yelled at in the presence of the underlings *he* must yell at, snorted when Mrs Kapur was well out of earshot, 'Who would dare attack Mrs Kapur? She and her dog would chew them up to little bones and spit them out in pieces.'

The police vans were still circling the area like many carrion birds. Well, two to be precise. I spotted Sweaty and Swarthy hanging around aimlessly on the premises.

Mrs Kapur, back from her constitutional, joined me in the park where I was watching the child bond with his friends over some major kickass Dragonball Z moves. 'You know the blood stains are still on the road, they haven't washed it off yet?' she hissed in the manner of one importing news of national concern. I shuddered appropriately and moued in horror.

I resolved not to take the road until I was sure said blood stains had been erased by someone or the elements.

'Does anyone know the family?' I asked. Concerned, naturally, about doing the neighbourly thing and offering one's condolences. And getting the inside dope on what could have really happened. 'Has anyone gone over to offer their condolences?'

We were, like any building complex residents, fanatical about going for condolence visits in a group. I decided to round up a bunch of women for a quick face show tomorrow morning, and looked for those willing to make the trip from amongst those in the park.

Every evening, these women trooped down ostensibly to grab a few rounds, but really to catch up on the local gossip. This batch of evening walkers weren't as focused on burning calories; they came down for the bonhomie promised by the gathering of the flock. They were markedly different from the morning walkers and runners. For one, they weren't in gym wear. The standard ensemble comprised hurriedly thrown together kurtis and track pants, and anything ranging from comfortable slippers to what could be kindly called PT shoes on their feet. They also comprised a markedly older demographic, who walked around in circles on the weaving jogging track for the better part of an hour and discussed various topics including cooking tips, school homework and the price of onions. Given that it had had hovered in the vicinity of Rs 100 per kilo a little while ago, the price of onions was definitely a worthy inclusion in the agenda.

Today, though, the primary topic of conversation across all age groups, bar the few who were babbling in the sandpit, was the murder most foul that had occurred on the back road. And the random corpse I'd had a close encounter with. Consequently, I was quite the celebrity du jour, with them crowding around me, determined to extract the minutest of details, including whether the fingernails of said corpse of slain man had turned black by the time I'd chanced on him, and whether, uggh, there was brain fluid oozing out of the bullet hole. For the curious, I hadn't noticed. It was night. I don't examine the nails of corpses in the dark. And I hadn't turned the body around to check for slimy grey matter. I had been too busy barfing at the side of the road. I didn't mention the barfing though. I'd like not to kill the image of me, tigress-like, coming across a dead body and holding my stomach and nerves together.

What was fuelling the excitement among the residents was the news vans parked outside the complex, with reporters wandering around the road like lost souls, holding their mikes out to random passersby in hopes of a sound bite.

I noticed that Urvashi—named after an apsara by her optimistic parents, but who had, in fact, sadly grown into someone far far removed from a vision of divine beauty—had, unusually for her, slathered on the lipstick. I panicked because I realised that I was sans make-up and outfit conducive for television appearances. I debated going up to change into sleek lycra instead of the faded kurti I had pulled over myself. It would be simpler, I resolved, to just jump behind a bush if I was accosted by anyone wielding a mike.

'No reporters within the complex?' I asked Urvashi.

'Nope,' she replied. Urvashi had been amongst the first enthusiastic souls to give her two bits of gyaan to a local news channel. She was now checking with all present whether they received said channel, and would they stay glued to the screen and record her appearance if they did.

I asked her to round up a few representatives of the building complex interested in paying a condolence visit the next morning, and hailed some packs of evening-walkers down, to get potential candidates for the same purpose. I needed to get more details about Mrs Jaiswal, and who better to share them with us than a bereaved

Mr Jaiswal, who would undoubtedly be in blubbering-with-sorrow mode.

The Saturday concluded as most Saturdays in suburbia do: with dinner at the nearest restaurant that doesn't require us to reserve a table. We aren't finicky about the restaurant. We just need a table and a waiter willing to serve us.

This evening though, Kabir had had his specifications. 'I wantu ead chikken kandoori, chikkin lollipok and fisfry.' This had us tearing our hair out for restaurants with a child-friendly ambience and a menu that included Chinese and Mughlai (apart from not requiring a reservation).

Thankfully, once within restaurant premises, the brat was fairly content with animal flesh from a single cuisine and, sated stomach, was keen to get back to his investigations, having hounded his father into playing his sidekick, aka Daya as shown in *CID*, while he played ACP Pradyuman.

He began his investigation by ordering his father to kick down the door to our house. Instead, the door was opened by the good key meant for the purpose and the miniature ACP Pradyuman was changed into night suit, and threatened into sleep.

I changed into my chocolate-coloured satin pyjamas, the one with the kind of luscious feel against my skin that induced all sorts of sinful thoughts, and dozed off faster than I could move a finger to put the seductive quotient of said pyjamas to use. The deep sleep didn't last. I slept the sleep of the disturbed, dreaming that I was crawling through rivers of blood and corpses as I struggled to get home to get to a bathroom because I desperately needed to pee, till the conscious mind took over and woke me up. I hobbled painfully to the bathroom. I didn't bother switching the light on. Thankfully, there was enough light streaming in from outside to light up the room dimly. And my eyes were now LASIKed into enough sharpness to avoid tripping over rugs and other such errant items designed to waylay the desperate night-time toilet trip-maker.

As I drowsily got back into bed, I thought I saw Sheetal Jaiswal, in her grey tracks and pink T-shirt, standing in the balcony outside my bedroom, her face pressed against the glass, looking in. She took up two frames of the sliding door. With little margin left.

I blinked my LASIKed eyes and looked again. Widened them, and let the tear film make for sharpness of the image. There she was, resplendent in her rotundity. All those years of pounding the pavement hadn't made a whit of difference, and therein lay the moral of the story about the efficacy of morning jogs, but I don't see the moral of the story unless someone puts it down in bold, forty-point-size font, and therefore I continue to step out for a morning run.

I gasped. Or rather, I opened my mouth to gasp, but no sound emerged. I patted the snoring spouse with a trembling hand. He continued snoring.

She didn't have her headband on, I noticed, with a vague start. It was like looking at a man suddenly bereft of the regal handlebar mouche you've always seen him with—face-naked, if you know what I mean. In the years that we had passed each other pounding the tarmac, Sheetal had always had her hair held off her face with a headband.

Maybe headbands were redundant in the afterlife; perhaps hair stayed grimly in place without the help of hair gel or serum. Maybe every day in the afterlife was a good hair day. That was a happy thought for me, considering that every morning I gave myself a fright when I caught sight of reflection in the bathroom mirror, panda-eyed, baggy-cheeked and bedhead to end all bedheads.

Then the fear hit me. Rather a delayed reaction. Was I seeing a ghost, or was this just my imagination being its usual overactive self. I poked the snoring spouse again, this time with a sharp, insistent fingernail, freshly filed the previous evening. The spouse, when in deep REM, would probably sleep through a bombing and an earthquake combined and get up wondering why the bed was that wee bit uncomfortable.

I opened my mouth but like MJ said, the devil took the sound away before I could make it. I was dry-throated and unvoiced. I poked the rather fleshy back of the spouse unkindly, and turned back to look again at the windows. The soft outline of Sheetal seemed to be fading away, looking at me with an expression that was the kind of mournful that automatically made you feel guilty for being alive.

The spouse grunted indecipherably. I poked him again. 'Whaaaaa?' He jumped up with the kind of start that folk reserve for when one has had a bucket of water tipped over one. I pointed at the windows.

'Look there,' I whispered.

'Whaaaaaa?' he went again, in tones loud enough to wake the dead. The child continued snoring blissfully between us, unaware of the ghosties looking in from the window.

I looked again. Blinked hard. There was nothing there but the dapple of shadows. No spectre of the newly-dead balefully staring at me, with a rather bovine expression that hadn't even begun to make me feel terrified in the way ghosts are supposed to.

Had I imagined Sheetal standing there? I raised a hand to my forehead. It felt quite cool and nowhere close to feverish levels. Had I really, truly and absolutely seen a ghost, or was I hallucinating? I blinked again. Furiously willing the tear film to clear my vision. My brain was probably frying itself with an internal fever and conjuring up images out of nowhere, I concluded.

'What is wrong with you, Kay?' said the man in tones so exasperated that had they dripped with acidic rancour, the bed would have had giant-sized holes in the mattress. 'Can't you let a person sleep in peace?' he concluded bitingly and settled himself back again onto the bed with the kind of ominous creak that indicated he would not take kindly to further demands to check out the premises for spiritual manifestations. He was back to snoring in his deep, rumbling tones barely his head hit the pillow again.

You would think a man would be curious about why he had been roused from sleep. You would think he might even be happy about being roused in the middle of the dark night, by a loving spouse all wide awake and alert. Not this man. This man will not be happy about being roused from his sleep even if the houris descend from heaven; what is a mere wife in comparison?

I breathed deep and I breathed hard. I gathered all my courage and felt it like a hard knot in my stomach. I felt my heart palpitating. Visions of the cyclone-hit room in *Poltergeist* spinning before my eyes, I pushed open the sliding windows and gingerly put a foot outside. The tiles on the floor of the balcony were cold. Where was it that I'd read about paranormal activity starting with a sudden sense of unspeakable chilliness? I shivered. I gathered my fraying courage and stepped out onto the balcony. I expected to be swept off into a vortex taking me to another dimension where spirits would berate me for not being appropriately respectful to them and scoffing proof of their existence even when they soundly banged doors around the house, and then insist on boiling me in otherworldly oil for eternity. My foot landed on dried pigeon shit and two pigeons grumbled noisily as they fled off the top of the air-conditioner.

Apart from the fleeing pigeons, all seemed calm and quiet, albeit chillier than was allowed on a December night in Mumbai. I felt a chill go up aforementioned spine. Chills go up my spine on a regular basis. Maybe I should just strap on a heating pad to my back on a permanent basis. Resisting the urge to head out further into the minuscule balcony, I turned right back, dropped myself on the bed, put my head down on the pillow and snored right back to the same river of blood-converted back road, and fought off the corpses, who by now had taken on zombie characteristics and were attacking me with a ferocity that came only from watching too many C-grade horror movies. The next thing I knew, it was morning.

Sunday morning. The morning of no 5.45 a.m. alarms. The morning meant for lying in and sleeping till the maids start ringing the doorbells plaintively, asking to be allowed in to do their work. Inevitably, as is the case on such mornings, the child will get up at 6 a.m., all bright-eyed and wanting to play. I tried in vain to get him back to supine position and maybe a couple of hours more of sleep. He climbed onto my stomach and prised my unwilling eyes open with pincer grip that doesn't seem to work too well when holding a pencil and trying to write alphabets.

'Mamma,' he asked, with all the curiosity of the one million questions always tumbling out of his mouth before you can get round to answering the first. 'Wen yu die yu become a ghos?'

'Not everyone,' I mumbled, and covered my face in the vain hope that it would fool him into going back to nod-land.

However, this is a child not to be deterred by sleeping moms or dogs. He will not let either lie. He peeled the covers back and prised open my right eye with a determined index finger and thumb move which should make it into the manual of Chinese torture methods. I swore on all that is holy that he would be moved out into his room the next night, damn all the ghosties lurking under his bed. He was unfazed. He would deal with the ghosties under his bed when he came to them. Now he wanted to know how ghosties came to be formed.

'Ask your father,' I muttered finally. The father in question was sprawled like a starfish, mouth agape, dreaming probably of a market zooming past all circuits and making a killing on NIFTY.

The child was made of stern stuff. He poked the father in the ribs, leading the man to jump up sputtering obscenities that made me remark strongly (but sleepily so I wouldn't be asked to handle child) that I would not stand for such language in the child's hearing.

'Pappa whu becomes a ghos wen dey die?'

Obviously, this question had been accompanied by action with intent to injure or maim. The look in the father's eyes was as far from paternal and loving as could be. In fact, murder was writ large in them. 'There are no ghosts, beta,' said the practical, unromantic father with as much calm as he could muster, turning his back to the child and effectively ending the conversation.

The child turned his attention back to me, and I solemnly pulled the blanket over my head again, thinking back to the very solid person standing in my balcony the previous night, trying to draw my attention. The solid person who was to all evidence, a ghost. A ghost of a person recently deceased on our premises.

The child climbed off the bed, and began pottering around raising Cain with various action figures on make-shift arenas which were originally meant to be study table and dressing table respectively. He moved out into the living room, where Jamuna was going through the morning routine before the cook came in, and demanded an unlimited supply of deep-fried smileys as breakfast, to which the girl began her wail on cue, 'Bhaaabhhhiiiii . . .' Yes. Good morning to you too. There is no rest for the wicked. If it isn't ghosts in the balcony, it is maids who do not feel the need to exercise their judgement and deny children unhealthy food even before milk teeth have been brushed by critters who do not have the sagaciousness to decide between healthy and unhealthy food.

I walked out to find a rolling-on-the-floor tantrum happening. He was picked up unceremoniously, his teeth scrubbed to sparkling whiteness, a mug of milk poured down his throat and Jamuna instructed to fry a couple of smileys to assuage the craving for deep-fried, fattening comfort food first thing in the morning.

All ye Food Nazis out there, kindly note this does not happen on a regular basis. My boy, he totally takes after me even in his food choices. I can just see him spending his adolescence sweating off his excess adipose in a gym. His father, on the other hand, has been blessed with a metabolism that keeps him in relatively good shape even though the only exercise he does is step out from the car and walk five paces into the office, and occasionally jump around in anger. I guess the overheating his brain goes into burns off adipose enough.

I myself decorously chewed on an apple. I had long stopped the tea on waking up thanks to Rujuta Diwekar and her sound advice on how she made Kareena Kapoor looked the way she did, and I was sure that if I squinted sideways and looked at my thighs at an angle of forty-five degrees in the mirror they were positively sylphlike, so the fruits and eating every couple of hours had obviously been working miracles. In any case, I needed the fructose to hit my brain and jolt me awake.

The morning passed in a haze of late breakfasts and discussions over the intercom as to whom all would go to offer condolences to Sheetal Jaiswal's family. The body had been cremated, that we knew already, the watchmen and helpers being the fonts of all information worth knowing on bodies dead or alive within the premises.

'Body ko fataphat jala diya,' said Murli, the odd-job boy who hung around the premises, washing cars and walking dogs. 'Posht motem se seedha electric mein daal diya, ghar eech nahin laye.' Surprising because we expected that the body would be kept in the morgue until the investigation into the murder was completed. But going by past experience, we figured Murli was probably right. He usually was. And his sources were normally unimpeachable. We suspected him of being a shapeshifter—probably morphing into a black fly on the wall to be able to find out the stuff he did. His secret, he claimed, was that no one noticed him around when they discussed things, and so they spoke freely. He was Ellison's Invisible Man.

Being cremated directly from the morgue is the way people who don't have families and loved ones go into the afterlife. Unmourned. Unprayed for. The elderly personages of the complex gathered around telephonically to tut tut over the glaring lack of respect for a dead person that had her disposed of swiftly as if she were a piece of meat. We, of the younger bunch, decided to gird our loins, metaphorically speaking, and trot across to offer our condolences.

Ever notice how difficult it is to go for a condolence visit for someone you don't really know too well? To start with, you have to start feeling sad. This automatically precludes watching funny movies before you set off. And then you need to tog up soberly. Which means cutting out the colour and the make-up. For someone like me who refuses to stick her nose out of the door if she is not adequately lipsticked, this can be difficult. I tried to resolve it by slicking on a nude shade, but it made me look positively vile and sent me shrieking back to the dressing table where I outlined them lips with a chocolate brown for some definition within the boundaries that the good lord had set for them. The biggest act of self-control, according to me, when given a free hand with lip pencil, is to stick to the natural outline of your lips and not be tempted to go just that wee bit overboard and end up with lips that look like you got collagen injected on a discount offer.

At the decent hour of 11 a.m., around five of us put on our white condolence and flag-hoisting and political meet purpose regulation salwar kameezes and appropriately mournful expressions and landed up at the E wing lobby, congregating like a flock of chattering seagulls. We took the lift up together in hushed silence though.

The Jaiswal door was spartan, bare as it had been received from the builder, with not even the token nameplate to denote the identity of the residents living within. The house opposite made up completely for the lack of ostentation on the surface of 1404 though. The door of 1403—which a huge frosted glass square on the side told us belonged to the Samras—had an artificial vine creeping all over its frontage, which was made of rough wood planks panelled to look like it was uprooted from verdant Swiss climes and transplanted into Mumbai suburbia, that too into a highrise from which the only spot of green visible was the tiny patch of garden.

In addition to the vines, a Panchmukhi Hanuman stood solemn guard over the wooden panels, just in case the delay in the supply of gas cylinders would compel a desperate lady of the house to strip the door of its rough wood panels in order to cook a meal for her starving family.

'Fifteen days now, and no cylinder. The Bharat Gas chappie is refusing to give a cylinder for anything less than 500 bucks,' said Ramola, standing morosely in a chikankari white kurta which had seen brighter days. She was from the B wing and perennially caught without a spare cylinder, being a working woman, ergo one who generally doesn't realise her second cylinder is running out, until it, well, does. 'I told the hubby yesterday, you get me a cylinder or you order food in, or you eat Cup-o-noodles. I'm not a magician.' We nodded in sympathy, not one of us volunteering our spare cylinder in these days of acute shortage and long waitlists, and gas delivery men with more attitude than a film star on set. Piped gas was a distant dream for us residents of this swanky complex because the roads were private and no digging through was going to be allowed.

I rang the bell. We waited uncomfortably for the door to open. I was acutely aware of the fact that the white churidar kurta I was wearing had been stitched for me in happier times, when the waist had some indentation, and would now probably need to be ripped from my body, and not in the sense you are thinking. It'll be fine, I consoled myself, as long as I remembered not to stop sucking my tummy in or take too deep a breath.

There was a long uncomfortable silence as the door remained unanswered. We waited, like good neighbours would wait, shifting our respective weights from heel to heel. We rang the bell again. And waited. And pondered what to do. 'Should we leave?' I wondered aloud. There was a limit to how much I could hold my tummy in; I could feel the stitches on the sides of the kurta start to give way.

'Arrey, phir kab aayenge? Let's finish it off now,' said Raji, never mind that our condolences were not expected.

The watchman had confirmed that the man of the house was at home, though. 'Poor man,' I said, 'he's probably in deep grief, and can't hear the doorbell. Shall we ask the watchman to call up on the intercom?' I have a bleeding heart.

Before we could act on this idea, the door was flung open, and a morose looking man, moroseness being determined by woeful eyes, the rest of the visage being covered by a growth of beard so violent, it hid all evidence of a face being under it.

'Yes?' he asked, in tones that harkened violins playing mournful dirges in the background. I gulped and swallowed, suddenly unsure about how to initiate a conversation with a man I didn't know, and who seemed at the point of bursting into tears.

'Yes?' he asked again in tones so woebegone, I almost began fishing in my fake Chanel mini white clutch for some tissues. The man, I noted, was bristly. He had tufts of hair bristling on the top of his head. Tufts of hair like a mottled carpet across his chest, visible beneath the thin T-shirt he was wearing, and his legs, bare and exposed below the shorts he had on, would have needed a sheep shearer to get all the hair off if he had been so inclined. The beard did not help matters. I wondered how his food managed to find its way past the bristles into his mouth; maybe he had a sonic radar fork-and-spoon set designed to circumnavigate the hair surrounding his mouth.

'Are you Sheetal's husband?' I addressed myself to the bristles. 'We actually came to offer our condolences.'

He made an indeterminate sound which could have been a choking sound of pain, or the sound of phlegm being caught in his throat. I clutched Raji for support. 'We live in the complex,' she piped in. Like that explained everything. It obviously didn't to Bristly. He raised one eyebrow questioningly. It reminded me of the huge villain in the old Chaplin movies with the fake beard and eyebrows, who was always left stuck in a door or a drum at the end of it all. He did not open the door more than the smidgeon he already had, which did not encourage us to murmur pleasant things about what a wonderful person she was. Which we were sure no one would refute, especially since assumed wonderful person was now cold dead, and of course no one speaks ill of the dead

'Did you know my wife?' he asked us in the same woebegone tone, which threatened to break into sobs any given moment. He looked from face to face questioningly.

'Err, no, actually, I used to meet her every morning when she went jogging, we went at the same time,' I stated, trying to establish a relationship worthy enough to necessitate a condolence visit.

'Hmm,' he said. 'Yes. She didn't have any friends. Thank you so much for coming. I'm not quite in a position to receive guests right now, as you can imagine, but certainly kind of you to come across.' And with a smile that would have done a heroine dying of cancer, saying her final goodbyes to her beloved proud, he gently closed the door. In our faces. My nose was millimetres away from needing corrective surgery to get back into alignment.

We shook our heads, shocked into silence at being thus summarily dismissed at the door itself. We moved away in gaggle formation to the lift. 'What a pity,' Raji said in frustrated tone of voice. 'He didn't even ask us in. I so wanted to ask him details about the murder! I don't know why we even bothered coming.'

Neither did we all. We returned to our homes, curiosity unslaked, discussing the strange Mr Jaiswal. Coupled with the little we knew of Sheetal Jaiswal, the couple seemed a strange duo indeed. Of course, we did feel a little sad for the man, he was obviously looking heartbroken; but still, it would have been nice to have been invited in and given the opportunity to show how deeply upset we were by the news of Sheetal's death. Clearly, both of them were definitely antisocial; it was—had been—a match made in heaven.

In the two years Sheetal Jaiswal and I had passed each other in the mornings, all we had done was crack an occasional wary smile at each other, not a single word had been exchanged by us. And for me not to exchange a single word with another familiar face was like a kid not feasting herself silly in a candy store.

Yes, it was true. She hadn't had any friends. What a miserable life she must have led: no friends, an antisocial husband, and weight that refused to shift itself.

When I got back home, the maid informed me that all the residents of E wing were being questioned, which made me feel a little better that I hadn't been the only one singled out for this dubious honour, merely because I had happened to pass Sheetal Jaiswal on her way out for her morning jog. I hoped she had conveyed this nugget of information to the snuff-rubbing doorjamb boy from the flat opposite who had been staring beady-eyed when the sweaty arms of law had walked into my apartment.

Lunch ingested and a short nap later, as was our norm, we draped ourselves in our Sunday casuals and trotted off to the clubhouse around 4 p.m., where the spouse and the child would swim in the pool till their skins turned into wrinkled-prune consistency and all the chlorine would ensure that the husband's hairline would reveal even higher levels of intelligence than God had intended him to have at current age.

I sat around in a deck chair, sipping a cold coffee. A woman needs her calcium. I do not swim. It has been many years since I dared be seen in public in a swimming costume. I will not dare be seen in public even with swimming costume with them thoughtfully-placed frills to camouflage cellulite-rippled thighs and behind. No matter how many sessions of lymphatic drainage I paid for at the local cosmetology salon, the thighs were going to have handles which could let the man pour from me if he so wished. Nevertheless, I was so going to ask about that procedure where they took out the fat lodged in the hips, thighs and assorted body areas where they have no business being and transferring said fat to areas of body which are desperate for it.

Talking about fat, 'Hey, Kay,' Meena tapped me on the shoulder and pulled up a chair to sit next to me. Meena was the kind of slim that made you believe she was moulded at the Barbie factory, without the topple-over chest assets.

She was all fresh and sparky in the way a person is after having sweated out almost all superfluous body fluids in a game of squash, followed by a nice long shower. Fresh-faced in a way that makes me want to pull out my compact and daub on some powder even though I have patted my pores down barely ten minutes ago. In the way that makes you wonder jealously if she is doing vile things like massaging placental extracts on her skin, and having the epidermis injected with hormones from aborted foetuses and other such unmentionable treatments which are whispered about but no one actually confesses to getting done.

'What's the latest on the murder?'

And who died and made me the official spokesperson for the investigating team, might I ask? 'No clue, really,' I replied, acutely aware that Meena's waist was approximately the circumference of one of my thighs. And that both her thighs together were the equivalent of one of my arms.

I was torn between wanting to shoot her in the head for being so unbelievably slim, and asking for her dietician's number. My last dietician had been arrested by the police for having piles of notes tucked under a mattress in a nondescript bedroom of her nondescript building in a nondescript suburb. In her waiting area, I had rubbed shoulders with Page 3-ites and Bollywood actresses. I'd been convinced she gave them some special plan because they all shrunk as if cling-wrapped, while the needle on my scales refused to go anywhere but north. I have broad bones, I console myself. I have a frame that, even if I whittle down to zero body fat, will need to go sideways through a turnstile.

'The police are still sniffing around in the area,' I added, something that was evident, seeing as the police jeep was clearly visible at approximately ten yards from the main gate. I wondered if I should mention seeing Sheetal

Jaiswal's spectre standing in my balcony, but then decided against it. Wouldn't do to be put in the same bracket as the loony bin candidates including the old lady from the ninth floor who spoke to herself as she walked backwards exactly five paces from the glass doors of the lobby entrance before gathering the courage to walk out. Tricking the djinns, that's what she whispered to the brat one day when he'd asked her in the clear, direct way we adults have forgotten, as to 'Wai yu're walking ulta pulta?' This was, of course, followed up by the second inevitable question, 'Whu'z d gin? Pappa has in d bar?' I, of course, had sputtered at the most age-inappropriate turn in the conversation and had nipped it in the bud then and there, and had ensured that it was never repeated by means of sharp insistent pokes in the child's back whenever it seemed our paths would cross with the backward five-pace walking lady.

'Two murders in two days is no joke,' Meena said, face appropriately creased with worry as she stretched herself comfortably in the chair. 'My calves are aching, I played for almost two hours today,' she sighed, referring to the squash game she never missed over the weekend, for love or money. I looked at the shapely calves stretched out for my inspection with much of the green tinge clouding my vision.

Meena had to go for an advance movie screening she said, later, mandatory attendance to get her mugshot in the party pages of celebrity-starved city supplements. 'And it's a kiddy film,' she grumbled pleasantly. 'But, that's part of the job definition, to be seen even if one doesn't want to see.'

Another familiar face, Rupinder Ahluwalia, from F wing, spotted us across the length of the pool and tripped over to join in the conversation without an express invitation. Rupinder is the sort who could barge into a heads of nation summit without an invitation and discuss the best way to make dahi bhalles. She is not the sort of girl who would have sat on the sidelines at a prom waiting to be asked to dance; she would have walked up to the most in-demand boy at the do and commanded him to dance with her. It was a mindset I admired. I was of the other persuasion. I would be the one who would hide behind pillars and hope no one would want to dance with me.

The sole purpose of Rupinder's current bonhomie was, of course, the implicit request for an introduction to Meena, which was duly done perfunctorily by yours truly, after which a full five minutes of gushing ensued in which she raved over a particular saree Meena had worn in a particular episode which had her take a gun and chase her evil brother-in-law around a pink and purple curtained set in menacing manner, to the deafening clanging of temple bells in the background. Meena graciously gave her the number of the in-house designer who would be able to give her knockoffs at cheaper rates, at which Rupinder squealed some more, and then lowered her voice to a conspiratorial whisper, almost like a channel had been switched on the telly. 'The lady who got murdered? E wing waali?' We automatically leaned in her direction like two strings had jerked us towards her. 'She and her husband didn't have any kids, na?' I nodded. Meena looked puzzled, wondering how not having kids was relevant to being murdered. I could understand her concern, she herself being unburdened with offspring, and also free of spouse. I had always envied her life, national fame, a career to die for, no one to answer to, and the freedom to call for takeaway every single day of her life. And I was sure Meena envied my life in a way I couldn't understand, and definitely did not want to understand on days when the child had me tearing my hair out in bunches and feeding the handfuls to the crows.

'Always fighting, fighting, fighting. My kitchen is opposite their bedroom,' she added by way of explanation, in case we assumed she had been sitting in darkened rooms with binoculars and a room full of monitoring screens. Living in a housing complex this tightly packed leaves you with no secrets. I resolved to drag the spouse into the bathroom the next time we decided to yell at each other. Or maybe we could fight via SMS.

'Day and night fighting. One day, they threw things and broke a window. Meri toh death hi ho gayi.'

We assimilated this information with the grave silence it deserved. Ah, well, couples do fight. Fighting was an essential part of coupledom. But breaking windows in the course of a fight was, to put it politely, a bit extreme.

The kids squealed and splashed noisily in the pool, with the kind of wild abandon that being in water brings to children who do not yet feel the cold dread of living in the shadow of murders, them being of a generation that has grown up on video games where success is rated according to the number of gruesomely decapitated bodies splayed on the screen.

The spouse did his laps with annoying precision. I looked on, and then looked away and ordered some more deep-fried stuff to comfort me. I am the kind of person whose idea of being sporty is to wear coordinated tracks and tees and sports shoes and then not do anything that will make me sweat off my make-up. I walk gently, I feel good. I wondered whether I could walk without being slit at the gullet tomorrow morning. I decided to risk it.

The sun dipped gently over the horizon, tingeing the sky a brilliant shade of orangey-red. We raised ourselves from the chairs we had got embedded in and kissed cheeks, promising to do lunch sometime soon. As we walked back through the complex full of squealing kids, football-playing teens, and groups of adolescents draped carefully over the cars parked in the compound engaged in high-voltage discussions of indeterminable nature, I wondered what Sheetal Jaiswal and her husband fought about so ferociously that neighbours could hear their raised voices. I wondered if any more women were going to be killed. Or any more men.

# CHAPTER 6

# IN WHICH I START
# THE WEEK BY USING
# PEPPER SPRAY

**T**HE NEXT DAY DAWNED BRIGHT AND EARLY with the infernal antelope beep on the mobile shrilling into my ear at 5.45 a.m. Like I always do when the alarm rings, I woke with a start and a heart that slammed against the back of my teeth. And then, slowly and sulkily said heart makes its way back to the vicinity of the rib cage. If there is ever a need for getting heartbeat back in an emergency, I recommend the antelope alarm. It will startle any soul back into the realm of the living. Maybe it should be standard resuscitation procedure in Emergency rooms.

'Shut the damn alarm,' the spouse said, opening one eye. He muttered nastily about my insensitivity in setting alarms at wake-the-dead volume so an honest man could not get his honest sleep. All of which I soundly ignored, this being part of the scripted dialogue between a man and a woman who have been married for over a decade. One is allowed to grumble without the other taking said grumbling seriously enough to actually alter the behaviour pattern that sets off the aforementioned grumbling.

I went into the bathroom and started in shock at my reflection in the mirror. Those weren't bags under my eyes, those were soft back suitcases I could pack and take on a transcontinental journey if I wished. With extra outfits to see me through any unforeseen events like a red carpet do. Where, of course, nothing I have will ever fit me. And I will need to run out to the shops, my charge card held aloft, shrieking at the salespeople to throw whatever they have in XL at me. Or whatever term they use for the size that means grossly overweight person who needs to enrol into fat farm immediately and be shrink-wrapped in cling film until the fat cells squeal in protest and disgorge their cellulite into the blood stream where they will no doubt race to my heart and clog up my arteries until I suddenly one day find an iron fist crunching up my chest. The bags, the bags. I looked like a worn-out lush. And were those lines on my forehead? Had no one sent that memo about delayed ageing to my forehead?

Okay. Breathe. Start with the basics. Brush your teeth, wash your face, pull on your tracks and sports shoes, tie your hair back. Breathe deep and set forth. Walk, run, walk, run, pound the pavement, feel the adrenalin flowing, watch out for dog poo. Sidestep said dog poo adeptly. Improves reflexes. Where can you get this on any treadmill, I ask you?

I let myself carefully out the door, with all the subtlety of an elephant trying to avoid the flower bushes in a box garden. The door, which was supposed to behave and gently click itself shut, decided to act up and slammed at volumes which surely would have had the spouse jump up and spew the kind of flowery stuff that would immediately get the child's attention, and be filed in child brain for future usage and hurlage at friends in park fight situations.

I scurried off down the eighteen floors, wondering whether I was being needlessly brave or totally foolhardy in deciding not to skip my morning constitutional.

I passed the watchman in the lobby, snoring open-mouthed, his head on the desk. A tad complacent, I felt, as the watchman in charge of a twenty-storey tower with eighty flats in the immediate vicinity of two just-committed murders. Oh, what the hell, at least if I get my throat slit, I will die a fit corpse, I thought.

The air was nice and crisp. Mumbai has the kind of winter that is over before you can say Jack Robinson, so it is best to enjoy it while it lasts. Plus, I *had* to justify the cost of those Reebok EasyTone shoes and those four coordinated sets of Juicy Couture tracksuits, including the one I was currently wearing in bright red velour with a nice zip front hoodie. With some random gold foil print up front in circular formation saying something I hadn't bothered deciphering yet.

I like hoodies. They make me feel, well, camouflaged from the need to smile needlessly at the people I don't really know too well, and don't care to pick up casual conversation with as I pass them. I can hood my eyes beneath the hoodie and be engrossed in my music as I walk briskly without needing to stop and make casual conversation with retired Mr Bose from the sixteenth floor on the state of acute neglect the premises have got into and how all the committee members are on the take from the various contractors and service providers and how we need to rise as one and unite against the committee and take matters into our own hands . . . by which time fifteen minutes of my walk time will have been chewed into and I will need to excuse myself and run straight into Mrs Kapur of the flaming white hair and the yapping white Pomeranian who will nip at my ankles while I dance gracefully trying to avoid having the legs of my pants punctured with insidious little holes that no amount of skilful darning can put together. And thank the Lord for the thick socks I insist on wearing.

Don't get me wrong, it isn't that I don't actually like making small talk, but when a girl's gotta run, she's gotta run. And I'm not at my best first thing in the morning. I need to work up to that jogger's endorphin high in order to be sociable. And that takes the better part of the hour. Small talk I reserve for later in the day when I am awake, alert and energised. And have a couple of cups of caffeine in me. Or something stronger.

Therefore, I now plug in the earphones, and walk run, walk run without looking up at what approaches me or who passes me. Given that a fellow jogger was recently approached by a knife with murderous intent, this might not be such a great idea I decided, and psyched myself into being alert, aware and keep my reflexes sharp. This meant keeping a watch on the folks around. I looked up and took stock of the situation around me. The total headcount on the road, barring the milkmen on their cycles and newspaper vendors straggling down towards the gates of the complex, was one.

I felt like a woman on a mission. I was the only one in the entire complex of seven towers who'd been brave enough to head out. I could feel my halo shining bright enough to eclipse the street lights. I was literally in the front rank for bravery awards. I had seen a ghost the previous night and I had not passed out in fear, nor gone into chattering shock. I half saw myself in red evening dress doing a Milla Jovovich in *Resident Evil*; I just needed a nice automatic rapid-fire kind of weapon to complete the illusion. Never mind, I would just have to settle for pepper spray.

I checked in the pocket of my hoodie for the the small lipstick-sized can of said item the spouse had so kindly got me from one of his umpteen work trips to foreign climes. 'Knowing you, I'd feel safer if you kept this with you when you go for your morning walks,' he'd sighed, and added, 'Why can't you just circle around in the garden? Would help me sleep in peace.'

Undoubtedly, he was right then snoring peacefully in his bed while I ran on roads stained with the blood of murdered innocents.

I could feel mists of air coming from my nostrils; it was that strange little chill that had set in these wintry mornings. The sun wasn't out yet, and the street lights cast uneven shadows. Parts of the road were unlit and dim. I kept to the side of the road, hoping to go unnoticed in case any suspicious type of person was still lurking in the shadows waiting to accost, rob and kill passing joggers.

I did not like this wariness that winter mornings brought on. But I liked that I had the road practically to myself. I could get used to it, not having to worry whether the folk behind me were giggling surreptitiously at my behind running to a beat all its own.

I shuffled the music on my iPod for some dance music to pep up my rounds and turned the corner. Unbidden, the thought came to my head that this would have been the approximate time I passed Sheetal Jaiswal at this same corner on Friday. And if there was still someone lurking around the darkened turn in the road, Sweaty and Swarthy would be lurking around the complex asking good folks questions about me. It scared me. People would discuss how I fought with the spouse loudly every weekend when asked to hurry up and get ready or we were definitely going to miss the start of whichever movie the man had bought tickets to.

You need to understand my concept of scared. Let's put it this way. I have watched every single horror movie ever produced from behind a judiciously placed cushion in front of my eyes. And with the volume on mute. And then I spend a week unable to sleep, sure that the strange sounds coming from the wall are not, in fact, the drip from the air-conditioning of the flat above but, instead, the very clear and present danger of the house taking on a life of its own and morphing into the Amityville terror of Mumbai suburbia and that soon my husband would develop insomnia and bloodshot eyes and try to push us off the balcony, and I would need to learn how to drive a speedboat. And learn to climb onto roofs. But this was getting way beyond the brief; right now, I just needed to concentrate on making it back to the complex gates without my head being sliced off my body.

I saw that a police van was stationed along the bend of the road. I passed it and noticed two constables stretched out full length within, their snores at a decibel level high enough to deter any lurking axe murderer or throat slitter, or pen-knife stabber. I knew immediately that I was safe on this road. The mere presence of the police van would have thieves and murderers dispense with the thought of making this a permanent hunting ground. And, I rationalised, no sensible murderer would come back to the scene of the crime, especially given that the police were posted in the immediate vicinity, supposedly doing the rounds.

But it was strange running alone on a road absolutely devoid of even the packs of stray dogs that usually roamed around with the swagger of territorial rights. My feet seemed leaden. And my running shoes—bought because they claimed to give one a J Lo-esque butt—were showing no impetus to get them feet to move to a snappier pace.

Maybe I was just too cold. I zipped up the velour hoodie to my neck, put the hoodie firmly on my head and tried to pick up pace. Not too much pace though.

Suddenly, a chill ran up my spine. If I were a spoor tracker in the jungle, this is the point where I would have 'frozen in my tracks' and sniffed the air; I would have paused in fight or flight. Or I would have peed my pants. I could see a figure standing at the distance, under the dim yellow lights of the streetlamps, dressed in grey and pink. And looking uncannily familiar. I blinked and looked again. The road was clear. I realised that the turning the figure had stood at, as if waiting for me, was just off where Sheetal had been found. I stopped. I had gooseflesh on my arms. And icicles poking my back. There was no one to be seen now. I blinked hard.

I have—as I mentioned earlier—chills running up my spine on a regular basis. When the mercury dips below twenty degrees Celsius in Mumbai, it is a clear indication to me from the good Lord above that it is now time to get the woollies out and aired ready for wearing. I am that person who sleeps in Mumbai's regular climes with a woollen blanket and socks on my feet. And I am the one who is known to have worn every single item of clothing in her suitcase at the same time when she was in a place where the temperature went below ten degrees Celsius. And then fought tooth and nail to appropriate all the blankets on the premises for sleeping underneath purposes and prayed in the night for the good Lord to not let one need to pee because hobbling to the bathroom and getting through multiple layers of clothing to relieve oneself in the cold would be agony nonpareil.

So, I was saying, a chill crept up my spine. I thought of a very strange thing as I passed the spot where Sheetal

Jaiswal had been found, throat slit. Dark stains of what I supposed were dried blood were still visible on the asphalt. The exact spot was just ahead of a blind turn-off from the main road, and in the direct line of view from where her apartment would be. So, in effect, if there was someone sitting by her bedroom window, drinking an early morning mug of java, they would have been able to see Sheetal turning into the road. And Sheetal being accosted by the mugger and being knifed to death. And they would also have been able to see Sheetal lying on the road, her blood flowing out of her, under the yellowing street lights.

And then, the fact that she lay bleeding for well on thirty minutes to an hour when the spot was completely visible to most of the building, to anyone who cared to stand out at their bedroom windows and breathe in fresh, smog-laden morning winter air was something that made me a little uneasy. And her iPod, they said, had been lying on the ground right next to her body. Untouched.

Suddenly, my sixth sense, which is generally always on track, sensed something behind me. Or someone. I could hear whatever it was keeping pace with me as I ran, the dull thud of the footsteps behind me running at exactly the same tempo. I could hear breathing—the kind of breathing done by someone who is running not out of choice, but out of necessity because the person you're after is running as well. Which in this case, was me. Little me. Helpless little me, with only a small can of pepper spray between me and an axe or pen-knife murderer.

My heartbeat quickened in a way it hadn't for a long time, not even when I happened to be on the same flight as model-turned-actor Arvind Singh, who—finding his exit from the aircraft being blocked by me gawping in most goldfish-like manner—had drawled, 'Excuse me, I'd like to disembark,' in his trademark baritone which had me smiling like a lunatic without actually registering what he was saying. I remember an airhostess moving me to the side like a stage prop while my head turned at an unseemly180-degree angle as he passed me with a half-smile, and strode out of my line of direct and peripheral vision. Yup. That was the kind of thump in my heart right now, but surely no Arvind Singh was keeping pace with me. It had to be the mass murderer with the most vile intentions.

I took a mental inventory of all I had of value on me. Why had I not taken off the jewellery I had on before setting off on my morning constitutional? An eternity ring, given to me on my fifth wedding anniversary. A diamond tennis bracelet—yup, you can wear a tennis bracelet even if you don't play tennis—bought to commemorate the birth of the brat. A pair of solitaire earrings and a matching pendant. Maybe I could convince the heavy-breathing follower to take them and spare my life. But the clasp on the chain was tricky and only the spouse was an accomplished master at getting it undone. Maybe I could convince him the chain and the pendant were of no value. Maybe he would cut my head off to get the chain. Maybe he wouldn't notice the chain under my hooded jacket. Maybe, he would, horror of horrors, strip search me or worse. I put the worse to the side of my mind, because Sheetal Jaiswal had not had strip-search or worse happen to her.

My hand went to the tiny can of pepper spray in my pocket, and closed round on it. I wondered whether to keep running or to stop and turn. I said the Hanuman Chalisa in my mind, with the awkwardness of someone who calls on the gods only in times of deep distress and doesn't really have the words down pat.

At that moment, a rush of affection surged for the spouse. If I survived this attack, I would be more grateful in a displayable manner when he returned home bearing gifts which score zero on the romantic scales but were evidently bought with much thought and consideration. Like the Pepper Spray Can. And the Talking Weighing Scales with a Very Loud Nasal Voice, bought so that I could weigh myself and not need to suck in my stomach and squint down to see what it said, and therefore not kid myself that I was actually a couple of kilos less than what them damn scales insisted I was. Of course, the Talking Weighing Scales were only used when no other human being was in the immediate vicinity. And at premenstrual bloat time, I have even ensured that the neighbours opposite us aren't at home in case the annoying nasal voice decides to carry through the thin walls into their home.

I gripped the pepper spray can firmly, like a woman with a plan. I am nothing if not a woman with a plan. I always have a Plan. And if that Plan doesn't work, I am always a woman with a Plan B. My Plan B was the speed dial on the mobile phone tucked away in the other pocket of my velour track pants.

I could hear the footsteps catching up with me; his breathing was loud now, heavy and forced. For a murderer, he sounded distinctly unfit. How did he make a profession of this? What could I do, I wondered, my hand gripping the can, ready to remove it and spray if I felt a hand touch me, which I did. That very second. A hand was placed on my shoulder.

A blast of icicles shot through my skin, and my stomach churned like a week out on rough sea. I stopped cold. And turned around with a swiftness I didn't know I had in me, and which the father, would have been delighted to witness, after all the years he'd spent in vain trying to instil a swift responsiveness in me which wasn't limited to fraction-of-a-second reaction time on spotting the 'On Sale' sign in shop windows.

I pulled the can out in a single, smooth motion and sprayed straight into the face of the person behind me. And when the language broke out, florid and familiar, I gasped in horror of recognition. The spouse was sputtering and cursing merrily as his eyes no doubt burned enough to give him first-hand experience of his gift. I gasped again and spewed apologies as he hopped in fury from one foot to the other. He coughed and coughed and spasmed, and bent forward and backwards in agony. I apologised profusely, as I tried to daub off the spray to agonised squawks of '@#$$%'.

Now was not the right time for me to start protesting about the use of foul and intemperate language, I guessed. Plus the guilt was bubbling over and spilling forth. My god, I had read this could cause temporary blindness. I yelled for help. Loudly. I wondered if I should yell 'Fire!', because I'd once read that folks come faster to help if one yells 'fire'.

A small straggly group of morning walkers and joggers seemed to appear out of nowhere and started gravitating towards us. Some looked distinctly aggressive on seeing female jogger seemingly accosting male person with unidentified substance. The spouse was still coughing and yowling in agony—the former preventing him from making the kind of death threats to me that I was sure he would have made if he was in any physical state to do so.

'I'm sorry, I'm sorry, let me wipe it off . . .' I cooed in my most billing and cooing voice, which has been known to douse many fires and ignite other fires at regular times. But this fire was not one which would be doused by cooing voice. I would need an antidote. I tried to help the spouse by turning him firmly in the direction of home, where I was sure a lot of washing off with soap and water would need to be done to relieve the pain. He threw my hands off him in anger. I didn't blame him. But then, how was I to know he would decide to pursue me on deserted roads. One doesn't expect husbands to pursue their own wives on roads. It is not done. It is unseemly and embarrassing.

'Anyone have water? Pani hai bhai?' he squawked in agony, hands outstretched, eyes closed with the burning. 'Kay, don't touch me!' he barked angrily and I sprung back hastily.

'Why were you following me?' I yelled back, offended.

'Dammit, I was worried,' he barked. 'You don't listen when I tell you to jog inside the building complex. You have a death wish!'

I mentioned to him that I was not the only one with a death wish—there were other people out and about. Including Mrs Kapur and her matching Pomeranian, who had arrived on the scene swiftly bearing a bottle of filter water. 'Arrey Kanan, yeh kya kar diya tune, bechare bhaisaab ki to haalat kharaab kardi,' she said concernedly. Yes, yes, yes, I made a boo boo, but this was not the right time to rub it in with salt. The expression in the spouse's now-open eyes did not bode well for me. They spelt out MURDER, in capital letters. Letters so capital that I knew I was going to be metaphorically dismembered the moment we reached home.

Colonel Singh, who ambled up wearing a striped, collared T-shirt tucked into shorts that were pulled up somewhere in the vicinity of his armpits, gallantly offered to help the spouse get back home. An offer I welcomed because carting along an almost six-footer, heavyweight, ex-sportsman, who would gladly wring my neck like a chicken, was not a prospect I looked forward to.

The Colonel took charge of the situation like a man who has taken charge of many situations. He informed us that water would do nada to ease the burning and made the spouse blink furiously to encourage the tears to flow freely. Then he frogmarched the spouse into the house. He called the local GP and asked what the course of first aid should be. He organised lignocaine gel for the burning skin and asked the spouse to bathe his face with baby shampoo, which thankfully was present in the brat's bathroom being used for the express purpose of shampooing brat's hair much to his squawking protests that 'I am nod a baby, I don wan baby shampoo. I is a beeg boy now.'

I digress; I stayed alive; even though the consensus was that I would be thrashed around like a rag doll by an irate spouse with hammer hands in tight grip around my throat.

I admire such people who take charge of situations and manage to make sense of nonsense. It's like women who can be counted on to have the really important things in their handbags, like safety pins and needles and threads for mending emergencies that might crop up with split seams and buttons that pop off shirts which strain at the chest. I, of course, do not fall into that category. I mean in the category of those who have said needles and threads and safety pins in their handbags. I've had my share of exploding buttons and splitting seams, the most famous amongst them being the one where I rose from the table after a hearty meal at a restaurant to have the button of the pair of jeans I had on fly off and ricochet off the wall, before finally coming to a halt after hitting a startled soul at the next table innocently contemplating the menu. I held the jeans together with goodwill and a prayer and made it back home that day without further incident. And anyway, there is no earthly way a pair of pants can get off me without my huffing and puffing and calling for help.

I am always woefully unprepared for emergencies. My concept of an emergency is forgetting to put in a brown shade of lipstick on a day when I am dressed in hues of beige and tan, and horrors, being compelled to slick on pinks or maroons on them lips. My handbag is full of essentials like gloss, mascara, sunblock, three shades of lipstick, liners, eye shadows, blush, compact. But ask me for something really important like a safety pin in an emergency of the sartorial kind and I will come up short. Ask me for all the wet wipes you want, and the mouth-freshening gum you need, and I will be of instant assistance. Ask me for a tablet to tackle a headache and I will be quick to hand you a choice. Ask me for a needle and thread and I will look at you like you were spat up from the earth, and still covered with primordial ooze. I am, to state the obvious, not a woman who is prepared for emergencies. Therefore, when confronted with emergencies, I look around in dazed blinking manner, hoping that someone else will take charge of the situation.

The child woke up as first aid was being administered to the spouse, who was now sporting a face that was an ugly shade of burnt toast. He bounded up to be in the thick of the action.

'Pappa, whachappent tu yer face. Is red colour. Like a tomato,' he said. This is not a child who knows the art of diplomacy. This is a child who has to learn that children should be seen and not heard. Making sheep's eyes at him to shut up did not have the required effect. 'Mamma,' he said, 'why yer making big eyes ad me?'

Thankfully, the maid took the hint and drew him away to his morning routine of milk and cornflakes and from thence to be slam-dunked into the bath, to emerge smelling of roses and baby shampoo to be dressed in school uniform and herded off to the school bus, which undoubtedly was honking down in the compound.

I quickly read the label on the can in the cold fluorescent light of the living room to figure out how I could further lessen the burning. The active ingredients in pepper spray cause distress to the mucous membranes, I remembered reading when I was first handed said can of self-protection. Milk and honey is good, I remembered even more vaguely, while the man sat on the couch and threshed around in uncomfortable anger, while icing his face with a chilled pack. He is unfortunate to be blessed with skin which even in normal course of action will react if he doesn't use hypoallergenic soaps and mild shampoos.

I ran to the kitchen and mixed quantities of milk with some honey and raced back to apply the concoction to his on-fire visage. And hoped it would mellow his on-fire mood as well.

'What's this?' he muttered, as I tried in vain to get him to keep still as I daubed the mixture on, all the while apologising profusely and in as servile a manner as I could manage. I don't do the servile bit too well, but I made an effort.

'Milk and honey, darling,' I answered, continuing the daub/apply routine. 'To lessen the burning . . .'

'Bleddy hell, now you're putting face packs on me,' he barked in horror. 'This isn't some beauty contest here, Kay,

I'm telling you, just leave me alone, or else . . . or else . . .'
He left the rest unsaid. I was not sure whether I was
supposed to shudder and quake in fear in my size six butt
toning shoes which have so not had the desired toning
effect on said butt, that I have been tempted to ask for my
money back.

I left him to his misery and went to have a bath and
then read my newspaper in peace, sipping on a cup of hot
green tea. There are few pleasures of life as calming as the
morning routine of green tea, sipped at in unhurried
manner. As the warm, aromatic unsweetened tea goes
down your gullet, you can actually believe that all is well
with the world, and all murderers have been locked away
behind bars. I wanted to check if the police had made any
headway in the murder investigation. Had they found any
suspect, any further clues, had they revealed anything to
the press? There was nothing in the newspapers about
either murder. Not Sheetal's. Not the Purple Satin Shirt's.

The spouse was on an enforced holiday for the day.
This added to his very bad mood. He spent most of the
day working from home and barking at his minions on the
phone. The day went by tip-toeing on eggshells and
making diving catches to prevent pins from dropping.
And, of course, avoiding all references to skin the colour of
burnt lobster.

# CHAPTER 7

# WHEREIN I NEED TO EXERCISE RESTRAINT AT A BUFFET COUNTER AND FAIL

**I** WOKE WITH A SINKING FEELING IN THE PIT OF my stomach the next morning, when the antelope alarm tone beeped loudly. What was it today? My wedding day? Had Mira's birthday passed unwished into the ethers yesterday? Was I scheduled for a gall bladder stone removal? Was it my Class X algebra board exam?

Ah no, I had to go into the child's school. For a Parent-Teacher meeting. My stomach began contracting in nervousness last experienced when standing outside the Class X examination centre for my algebra paper, suddenly having blanked out of every single equation learnt and convinced I was going to turn in an answer sheet that was spotless, apart from the embellishment of my seat number.

The spouse opened one still-red disapproving eye. 'I hope you're not planning to go on the roads again today,' he muttered, before turning onto his side, every pore of his body oozing the kind of disapproval that has a loving wife begging to gain favour after almost blinding spouse the previous day. For me this meant telling the walls in general that I was going down to the PARK. I could be found on the jogging TRACK. And if there was any doubt about my whereabouts, a quick glance from the balcony should confirm my presence there. And I threw in a little aside about how he should stop being stubborn and take himself to an eye doctor rather than having everyone jump miles away from him thinking he's spreading joy and pink eye around.

Doing the rounds in the park is strange. To start with, the lights are switched off. What? Electricity is expensive. And earth hour and all that. So one feels like one is running around in a womb. And then, the track is round. Not a perfect round, more elliptical to be honest. Walking in circles is not something that makes for a good exercise session. And running in circles is what one does naturally through the day anyway, so to start the day doing it makes absolutely no sense. I began feeling faintly dizzy three laps into my routine. But I put my head down to the ground and pounded on.

The morning was dark and dull. A sort of pallor hung over the day like it knew exactly that today was the morning of the Parent-Teacher meet at school. I would rather go hunting for Count Dracula's remains in dank and dark Romanian countryside than attend a PTM. It is a very scary thing, this Parent-Teacher meet. Obviously not for them parents who have spawned child prodigies of the type you see in health drink ads, who are always taller, sharper, stronger, cracking complicated algorithms on blackboards and assembling robots, and getting coloured belts in various martial arts. I'm referring to parents like me, who have children who refuse to acknowledge that alphabets put together make words, and that writing of said alphabets is an acknowledged means of communication. And no, being sent to the naughty corner is not a matter of pride and puffed rooster chests to be recounted to all and sundry in the evening at the park.

This fear of the PTM is exclusive to parents like me, who know that this is on the Richter scale of traumatic life events, on the level of tooth extraction without anaesthesia or having to wade through a muck pool wearing your Savio Jon linen drawstring pants. You go in shaking like a leaf, knowing that the child you have raised is a wonderful, original, inventive, creative genius in the making, but unfortunately have nothing to prove this with when confronted with sheaves on sheaves of assessment sheets which state that the child has managed to break every known grammatical and spelling rule, and that the handwriting used to churn the stuff out is reminiscent of a line of recalcitrant ants crawling across a field spilled with sugar. I've tried telling the teachers that the most sought-after doctors and neurosurgeons have unreadable handwriting, and that anyway by the time the child actually gets to the stage where he needs to give in assignments, print outs will probably be accepted forms of submission in schools. I've told them not to worry their pretty heads about his handwriting so much as try to get him to sit still and pay attention to what they are supposed to din into his head.

School to the child is a place where he goes to engage in training to sharpen his combat skills. The standard conversation with the child post his return from school goes thus on an average day: 'Kabir, what did you do in school today?' This asked while tiffin and lunch boxes are being summarily inspected for tell-tale evidence of being chucked or distributed rather than ingested.

'Fusht I hit Arman,' he replies, naming the hapless focus of his unwanted attentions. 'An den I pushed

Ronak. An den Miss tole me tu sid quiedly in d notty korner.'

I gasp in horror. 'Did you get the time to do any studying in the midst of all this?' I ask the fruit of my womb.

'Nope,' he replies.

At least he's honest.

I console myself that this is not the time to study. After all, he is still a pre-primary kid. There is time enough to get out into the world and earn his degree.

I practised my lines as I did my rounds in the park. 'Yes, he is a little high-spirited.' 'No, no, he does pay attention at home, and sometimes he can even sit for an entire fifteen minutes on a single task.' 'Yes, yes, I can imagine, I will tell him not to run around in class and to stop pulling the girls' ponytails.' And finally, 'Thank you so much, I know he is soooo very difficult to handle, but he really adores you.' And run out of the class room before I get sidetracked into listening to declamations on how exhausting it is to control him when he has a temper tantrum. And I am not even attempting to meet his sports activity teachers.

As on days when the occasion scares the lunch out of me, the biggest question is always the 'What Shall I Wear?' one. This question was already on the blackboard of the mind, demanding an answer instantly. A question that had me mentally emptying the contents of my wardrobe onto a virtual bed and sorting through the pile, and rifling through the drawers filled with shoes and bags. If there was ever a fire in the building, I would be the one not grabbing my important documents, but running through flames to salvage my shoes. And maybe one handbag while I'm at it. Or two. And maybe a pair of sunglasses. Aaargggh. Maybe

I would be wrestling down the stairs with the entire wardrobe.

What should I wear to the PTM? What? What? What? I stood in front of the virtual wardrobe, rapidly scanning its contents for something that could take me through a Parent-Teacher meet without looking like a bimbette on the prowl for a sugar daddy and yet chic enough to be worthy of the ladies' lunch I was headed to later. A ladies' lunch with my ex-college gang, or what was left of it back here in India, given most of us had dispersed to foreign climes clutching our MBA degrees and work-experience certificates.

It was a crisp day; maybe a white linen pant suit with matte gold python heels and a coordinated matte gold Guess tote? And coordinated gold rimmed sunglasses? Would gold on white be too blingy, ladies who lunch type? But I *did* have a lunch scheduled at a to-die-for Chinese place; the old girls gang had wisely decided to throw diets to the dogs and opt for the totally sinful buffet spread.

Or should I wear a nice pair of well-fitted indigo denims with a white shirt and carry along my tan ostrich-finish Hermes Birkin rip-off. Simple yet chic. Thank god for rip-offs and trips to Malaysia and Bangkok to regularly replenish my stock.

I wondered whether I would need to fortify myself with alcohol before going to the PTM. Or keep the alcohol for later, to console myself that the child was only following in his father's august tradition of being a late bloomer. I had, after all, been the proverbial bookworm through my childhood. The result being spectacles so thick that the centre of my face had been squeezed into miniature if anyone looked at me straight on. Until contact lenses and then Lasik came along, I was the geek. Then I discovered shopping and make-up, and how a swift dash of eyeliner can make beady, round eyes so much less accusatory that I could actually fix an eye on someone and not have them squirm in their seat and confess to a murder they had not committed within a few seconds.

As I pounded the jogging track, I wondered if I could convince the spouse to accompany me to the PTM. Thinking back to the lobster face I'd seen before I had stepped out of the house, I knew I was not, by any stretch of the imagination, in a position to make any such requests. I looked at the buildings encircling the park and felt like I was on display for any random morning tea drinker to rest his bleary eyes on. Not that I was a sore sight for eyes. The body was clad in lycra-fitted pink tracks and a grey and pink hoodie. And in honour of Sheetal Jaiswal, I'd even tied my hair back with a matching pink scrunchy, remembering to lay out the scrunchy along with the tracks and the hoodie the previous night. Planning, woman, planning. If I got the morning look right, surely I would get the rest of the day right.

I ran the last few laps around the track, feeling the wind hit my face. I glanced up at the buildings again and noticed two figures standing in the balcony of E 1404, the living room balcony which overlooked the park. A man and a woman. The man was Bristly. The dark shadow of his beard was distinctive enough to stand out in the morning gloom. The woman was unknown. Young. A face I had not cast my eyes on before on these premises. That much was clear even through the morning smog.

They stood in pleasant camaraderie, both drinking cups of what seemed like some hot and refreshing beverage. And Bristly did not look like a man who was grieving the gruesome death of his wife barely a couple of days ago.

Bristly looked, if anything, like a man enjoying his cup of morning tea. Just then, he turned his head and looked at me. I looked away swiftly, guiltily. But, like a magnet, my eyes were drawn back again to the balcony. Now, standing calmly, looking down at me, in the same clothes she had on when she was killed, was Sheetal Jaiswal. And the front of her grey T-shirt was stained with what could only be blood.

I stopped in my tracks. Drew a deep breath and looked up again. There was no one in the balcony now. But I had seen her standing there, crystal clear. I blinked my eyes; obviously I needed to go for my annual eye check-up before I started doing a 'I See Dead People' routine and shocked the living daylights out of my stolidly practical spouse who would then have no option but to commit me to the loony bin, where I would have to wear terribly boring clothes of standard regulation uniform and have no access to a beautician. And no access to a mall either.

I closed my eyes, then opened them and looked full around the track. No dead people. Two elderly ladies shambling around. One nubile nymphet racing around at Usain Bolt speed. One paunchy creature racing around the track with sweat pouring down his face. And moi. No one seemed to be remotely in shock at the sight of people risen from the dead.

My half-hour of running done, the thigh muscles squawking in protest, the butt all popping runner's high endorphins, I returned home. Sipping on the tea thoughtfully prepared by the woman I worship most in the entire world, aka, the cook, I read about the further findings on the murders, now relegated to small paragraphs tucked away at the bottom of the city pages. The man we had found on the back roads had been a small-time actor and a part-time gigolo, the article said.

Unsavoury business was hinted at as the cause of his murder. The police suspected he had been blackmailing some highly-placed customers for movie roles. No suspects had been arrested though. The police seemed pretty certain that the two murders were not related, said the report. I take everything that comes in the newspapers with a pinch of salt. A mega pinch of salt. In fact with enough salt to spice up the oceans.

The child was packed off to school, but not before he insisted he wanted to gel his hair and spike it up aka Ben 10. I assured him that such fashion adventures were best reserved for birthday parties and other exciting events rather than wasted on unappreciative class teachers. Especially since it would draw attention to the fact that he was long overdue for a haircut and his hair had by now circumvented his collar and was somewhere in the vicinity of his shoulders. Blame this on the husband. He does not allow haircuts. If we'd had a daughter, I am convinced he would have hired armed bodyguards to prevent me from getting the child a haircut. For Kabir too, unless the hair reaches such levels that the child comes home with it tied off his face with a rubber band by the class teacher, and an express note in the diary about unacceptable lengths of hair, I was not allowed to take him to the men's salon. I was in charge of the haircuts, because the spouse does not believe in them. This is a man who spent a few years with his hair at shoulder-length, channelling his inner Feroz Khan or cave man, whichever way you choose to look at it. Need I say more.

The child was dandy enough to spend hours in front of the mirror combing his hair into 'cool' styles aided by hair gel and water. I have never seen him devote such single-mindedness when it came to getting his homework done in time. But let his hair not fall in the precise parting or spiking he required to look just like Ben 10 or Kevin Eleven or whoever it was who currently made his world spin, he would go right back to the drawing board aka the dressing table mirror and waste the better part of the hour until he managed to get it to look just right. I admired this persistence to reach perfection in his appearance. I used to be like that. Agony was nail polish not applied precisely and to perfection. Today I sit back like a beached whale and have a little girl with the bone structure of matchstick-proportions apply said nail polish to fingers and toes, and promptly slip feet into slippers to leave deep gouges in freshly-applied paint.

Kabir is a little different from the rest of the children his age. For one, he has a tough time paying attention to a single activity for more than five seconds. For another, his idea of fun is to get into kickboxing matches with other kids of his age and persuasion. This is a child whose idea of fun is ripping pages off the wonderfully illustrated books I bought him in piles in the early days when I still had hopes of him becoming a reader, and casting them off from the windows to see them float down, blown helter-skelter by the wind currents. Maybe there was a scientist hidden somewhere within that brain. Maybe there was a dancer. Or maybe there was a Bollywood actor. Right now the last seemed the most likely. He spent much of his waking day watching Bollywood songs on a loop. And quite fancied himself as a clone of Ranbir Kapoor. He sure had the skinny frame to start with. He had even changed his name to Kabir Kapoor. We hadn't done it in the gazetted formal way though. We were still waiting for the phase when he might want to change his surname to Khan. Officially. Till then he kidded himself he was a Kapoor. And ergo, destined to be a film star.

Sometimes I felt I was letting him grow like a weed. He didn't go for a single extracurricular class while the rest of his classmates were already enrolled in phonics, vocaboom, mental math and the like, and spent half their day racing between classes. Kids were on a race track these days, being groomed by their parents into being perfect at everything. Kids who could barely walk were experts in skating, swimming and had even mastered some martial art. The brat, on the other hand, was currently just good for street-fighting. If nothing, he would grow up to set up shop as a Hire-A-Goon.

I could just imagine that other parents of kids who had been at the receiving end of said street-fighting were waiting with red carpet rolled out for me, the Parent-Teacher meet being the one opportunity they would get to bring their pleas to authority figures, namely me. And the class teacher would also be waiting, with bated breath, to rattle off her list of issues with the brat. Maybe I should just wear armour and ear-plugs.

The husband had taken himself and his skin into the shower, in what seem like preparation for a day at work, with his clothes laid out neatly on the bed, down to the tie knotted just so, and the briefcase and laptop kept by the door for our driver, Samir, to take down to his car. He drove himself to work most days, except days when he had meetings in south Mumbai. He had no meeting today, I knew, since the blazer hadn't been kept out to be carried into the car. Ergo, I could be driven around.

'I'm still looking like burnt toast,' the spouse whined as he emerged from the shower, where he had no doubt spent the better part of the fifteen minutes examining his face from every angle. I consoled him with as much sincerity as I could muster about his handsomeness not being marred, and about the new look making him look all tanned and rough like a desi version of Indiana Jones, and left it at that. I had to get to school within an hour.

I wondered if I should mention seeing a ghost to the spouse. Given that I'd had multiple encounters with the deceased Sheetal Jaiswal. But he might frogmarch me off to a psychiatrist who would decry some brain chemical imbalance and dope me into a state of drooling imbecility. I wondered if I should mentioned seeing Mr Jaiswal with a strange woman in his balcony, having an early morning cuppa of the stuff that cheers. I finally decided to keep my thoughts to myself, and Google apparition visions when I got myself back from the PTM and the lunch. The thought of the lunch was distracting enough to take my mind off ghosts who popped up at the oddest times possible.

I got myself bathed and dressed quick as I could, given that the crisp white shirt I had in mind had suddenly, inexplicably, shrunk in storage and was in danger of popping a button or two and had to be replaced by a shift top with no button, and left, a growing knot of unease settling itself firmly in my stomach. I consoled myself with the thought that I had an entire buffet waiting for me once I finished the PTM, and I could eat to my heart's content comfort foods which would soothe my troubled soul. And I would have friends around me, friends who would not look at my heaped plate from the corner of their eyes or raise a single eyebrow when I tottered back from the buffet counter with the plate heaped to eye level for the umpteenth time, but instead would pat me on the back and exhort me to join an eat-all-you-can contest and try for a Guinness record for putting away the maximum amount of food in the minimum amount of time.

I love my food. I love buffets. When the two come together, especially after times when I am emotionally drained and hurting, like this, when I have had to sit through half an hour of being told why the child is well on his way to delinquency, and why I should report any signs of strange behaviour including pulling wings, legs and antennae off insects, and any tendencies towards arson to the school counsellor immediately, I need food that was deep fried, and desserts which are steeped in sugar.

The pleasant-faced Chinese girl who was manning (or should that be womanning?) the reservation counter led me to where three of my BFFs were waiting. I pushed the Tom Ford Samantha bug eyes I was wearing to the top of my head, where they would perform the very important function of making me look chic while keeping my hair from falling on my face and impeding access of my fork to my mouth.

The girls had already laden their plates with steamed momos. Tanaz, she of the Parsi antecedents and perhaps the only person in the whole wide world who can eat me under the table and go back for seconds, was attacking her plate with what seemed like a two-handed effort and the kind of grim relish only a food lover can empathise with. She nodded briefly in acknowledgement of my greeting while the rest stood up to cheek kiss.

We trilled our collective, 'You're looking gooooooood! You've lost weight! What ARE you doing?' to each other, and basked in the afterglow of being presumed skinnier than we really were.

'Your neighbourhood is damn scary yaar, I was reading about it in the papers,' said Ekta, who mournfully makes the trip down to the suburbs from south Mumbai once a month under much duress and threats of being cut off from us, her college gang. Ekta, a good Marwadi girl from Juhu, married old south Mumbai money and now lived at Marine Drive, in one of the elegant art deco buildings with a sea-facing bedroom, where we were not allowed to enter with our shoes on for fear of bringing in soil and other pollutants into the sanctified environment.

'You're a good one to talk,' I replied, bristling at the implied slur to suburbia. 'You have terrorists take over your entire part of the city for gun-battles, and you tell me two murders make my suburb dangerous?'

Ramola, nee Shah and now a perfectly respectable Mrs Bhatia, convent-educated expressly to up her stakes in the marriage market, and consequently married into a diamond trading family, was a walking advertisement for the family business, and now attempted to distract me by flashing a ring with a stone so monstrous, had it been any larger it could have applied for small planet status. 'Lookit,' she trilled, in full-on distract mode. 'My anniversary gift.' I got lost in the reflects from the million facets and stared in pure lockjawed, goggle-eyed envy. I made appropriate appreciative noises that sounded half way between appreciation and pure green jealousy, and then moved swiftly towards the buffet counter which had been calling out my name in dulcet tones, making it hard for me to concentrate on any conversation that was happening.

This buffet had been billed the longest one in the suburbs, and reaching it I knew just why wearing pencil heels to lunch was not a good idea. The counter snaked around the entire circumference of the restaurant; it was so long, dedicated diners would have to hire little golf carts to go around to the end to check what was available for dessert.

If only I had skipped breakfast, I berated myself, I could have shovelled more into my stomach and not lived in fear of belching in a public situation. Ramola wafted next to me at the counter, her plate barely smirched with a smidgeon of fettuccine in some low-fat sauce she had asked for at the live pasta counter. 'Today's my cheat day,' she informed me and the rest of whoever cared to listen at the counter, patting her washboard flat stomach with her free hand in emphasis. 'I'm on a personalised high protein diet for a month, can't have any carbs. My dietician is very, very strict. I have a detailed recall chart, she just knows when I fib.' Oh yes. That explained the pasta. And the quantity. Ramola was the diameter of a single thigh of mine. I almost hid my plate behind my back and edged away from her.

'You *must* give me the number of your dietician,' I said, knowing it was expected of me. No harm in getting yet another consultation. One never knew which diet it was that would finally make me sylph-like enough to chuck out all my kaftan tops en masse.

She lit up. 'And I have a fabulous woman who comes home to train you, thrice a week. See,' she put up the arm not holding the plate and shook it around for my perusal. Zero jiggle. Bleddy awesome. I clicked the jaw back into place. I thanked the Lord mine own batwings were hidden in a full pair of sleeves.

'You must give me the number of your trainer,' I cooed. The joy on her face was close to bursting levels. I had paid her the ultimate compliment. I thought she might jump up and click her heels in Mary Poppins' manner.

'Kay,' Tanaz looked up at me as I returned to the table, 'Why aren't you back to work now that Kabir is older?' Evidently, it was a question she had been itching to ask me for a while.

It was a question I had been asking myself too, and when I was being honest with myself, the answer was that I just wasn't too keen to move away from the creature comforts of enough time on my hands to do what I pleased. To scurry through the day, rushing through meetings, presentations, conferences and traffic wasn't an enticing option. I'm good at dodging this question though, it was one the spouse had cornered me with a number of times.

'Can't find anything worth my time. Tell me about your new guy,' I countered deftly. Tanaz, the eternal romantic and currently the only unmarried person in our gang, was newly in love. When she wasn't eating at buffets or falling in love, Tanaz handled the marketing for a beauty product that promised to have men walking into walls just looking at women who used the aforementioned product. Tanaz herself confessed to not using said product. It made her break out, she said in hushed tones, swearing us to secrecy over her betrayal of her brand. It being a working day, one assumed that she had managed to slip in a store visit at lunch time to make it to this lunch.

'I'm meeting him for dinner today,' she fessed up, whipping out her iPhone and taking us through around one million images of a droopy-eyed chappie. Ah. New love, that makes a frog a prince.

Tanaz and I were the only two who gave the buffet the attention it deserved. Calorie restriction is not something I am good at, especially at buffets. I am known for my affinity to buffets. I'm sure there's a secret conclave out there where managers plot how to keep me out of their restaurants when buffets have been laid out. I bet the concept of Kill Them With The Starters came up as a counter-attack for people like me, who can be counted on to empty out the heated containers of all that they contain. Starters. Deep fried. Steamed. Grilled. Running down the entire length of a table, so that by the time one finishes moving from dish to dish, filling up one's plate, goes back to ingest what one has piled on, and then returns for seconds, the feet are aching from the walking, and the stomach is bursting from the stuffing. So one needs to drag oneself with a real determination up from the chair and onwards towards the main course, and then having done the main course, the hired help has to lift one up and propel one towards the dessert because, of course, how can you even think of skipping dessert. Blasphemy. I have been known to sit for a good half hour, allowing the meal to settle a bit to make room for dessert. I am not called Buffet Queen for nothing. It's a title I have earned through some tough eating. I take my title seriously and am prepared to defend it to death. Probably caused by my stomach bursting.

Tanaz came up for air and for her second round. 'Try the crabs,' she urged, when she took a breath from shovelling the edible stuff into her mouth. 'They're to die for.' I declined gracefully. I have no courage when it comes to eating crustaceans in public. Not since the last time I had tried to cut a crab claw at fancy restaurant and it had landed with a splash in a soup bowl belonging to a lady seated at a table on the far end. She had fished it out and waved it around like it was radioactive. 'Who belongs to this?' she had yelled, and my cheeks had flamed to levels of shining bright redness that could guide a ship into port on a stormy night. Needless to say, I have stuck to simple fare since, dishes that yield to gentle ministrations of fork and spoon and can be transferred to the mouth with minimum fuss. Much protesting later, we found ourselves seated, eaten and sated, discussing murder all over again. Maybe murder made for a good digestive.

'No murderer apprehended yet, right?' said Tanaz, who was spooning into her third chocolate mousse with all the delicacy of a bull stampeding through the streets of Pamplona. 'Strange—no robbery, no reason for murder. Why would someone murder a random woman for no motive, unless there is some motive we don't know about?' Tanaz was also very good at solving crossword puzzles and Sudoko.

'Could be the shoes . . .' I replied, thinking hard. The assemblage looked on wide-eyed.

'What shoes?' asked Tanaz eagerly.

'They found the body wearing some strange gent's shoes and not the jogging shoes she normally wore every day, shoes I saw her wearing in the morning. Maybe someone killed her for her shoes.' The table erupted in spontaneous laughter, drawing bemused gazes from those in the immediate vicinity trying to concentrate on their meal.

'Be serious,' I was admonished sternly by Tanaz, now tunnelling through the ice cream.

'It's strange that a woman gets murdered on a road that has other joggers and doesn't scream when someone attacks her,' mused Ekta. 'If she *had* screamed, surely someone would have come to see what was happening? It isn't so deserted at that time in the morning, is it?'

Trust the quietest amongst us to come up with this, while we were all discussing trivial details like the amount of blood that would flow from a knife wound to the neck. Unless, of course, the attack had damaged her vocal chords, leaving her incapable of screaming. Maybe a thin, rasping screech had emerged. Not loud enough to attract any attention. Maybe she had been chloroformed in the best thriller television serial tradition.

I thought about this. I thought hard. Had Sheetal Jaiswal been too shocked to do anything when she saw the knife coming at her? Or had it been a quick slit of the throat from behind, something she had not seen coming? Or had she been running, like I do, lost in the iPod and the list of things to do for the day, unaware that someone was lying in wait for her to turn the corner before he could strike.

We moved off to our respective homes, after much hugs and air kisses and promises to get together with the husbands and kids, and current man du jour in the case of Tanaz, in the near indistinct future, having exchanged numbers of dieticians, personal trainers and facialists.

As I sat splayed in the car, having been helped to my feet and to the car by friends and thankfully not needing to be golf-carted out of the restaurant, my thoughts returned to the pieces of the Sheetal Jaiswal jigsaw puzzle that didn't really fit. And the very real spectre of the deceased person who seemed to be around everywhere I turned, glaring at me balefully, like she expected me to take action and haul the guilty off behind bars.

I decided to pick the brains of school friend-turned-private eye, Runa Bhattacharjee, as advised earlier by common backbencher school pal, Mira. Runa, otherwise known as Rune the Prune, for reasons that had nothing to do with her powers to make bowels move, rather more for the perpetually disapproving pursed lip look she favoured. We were an evil bunch of pre-teens. We handed out nicknames with the disaffection of the age that only judged a nickname by the amount of people it could lay low by bouts of uncontrollable laughter.

I jabbed a square tipped French manicured talon at the Blackberry. 'Darling Kay,' Runa growled. 'What is it you want from me now?' Trust Runa to be so, well, disarming.

'I want you to help me solve a murder.' I could do disarming as well as she could any day.

Runa laughed in the high-pitched Janice laugh she had before it became the Janice laugh. The kind of laugh that makes you wince and edge away to the furthest recesses of the room. 'Meet me for coffee tomorrow and we'll discuss it.'

I didn't really need convincing. The next day lay vacant and bare in front of me, and I dreaded that I would need to fill it in with a mindless shopping expedition. Not having a plan for the day is always scary. It leaves you feeling vulnerable and exposed to the fact that you really do nothing with your day. It makes you want to book salon appointments and get talked into doing crazy things with your hair to while away a few hours. I once emerged from just such a dull day with a perm that was, I shudder at the thought, with no malice to those who have such hair naturally, an Afro. I spent the better part of the next six months trying hard to popularise the headscarf as a fashion accessory.

So, coffee it would be tomorrow. Coffee which would be drunk while murders were discussed. And Runa would succeed in making me feel around four feet ten and back in pigtails in the way only she can.

# CHAPTER 8

# OF FEMALE DETECTIVES AND MY INITIATION INTO THE CLAN

**T**HE MORNING DUTIES DISPENSED WITH, I took myself in leisurely manner to the coffee shop two suburbs away where I had planned to meet up with Runa. I had not dressed up for the meeting, because Runa is the kind of woman who would snort if she felt you were objectifying yourself in the male eye. And this to Runa could include anything from a slick of eyeliner to a glimpse of cleavage.

It was hard on the world to see me in such drab costume, but the world would have to lump it. Runa is not the kind of woman you got on the wrong side of. No sir. Runa was the kind of woman you call at midnight and take along with you when you have a couple of goons you need bashed up to within an inch of their lives for eve-teasing. Runa is tall, built in a manner generously termed as stolid and dependable by men who would not like to, in any manner, cause her to get irate, and held a belt of some colour in a martial art that was not made popular by a song composed by our very own home-grown Biddu

Appaiah. She had the piercing keen gaze which could impale you to the spot like a fluttering insect pinned down to a surface by a sadistic child, the kind who grows up to set fire to random rundown warehouses.

She also had an affinity for weapons and spoke casually about the khukri in her rucksack, and the umpteen occasions when she has had to employ it in the course of her work, which had me unconsciously edging away from her, almost toppling over the edge of the narrow pavement which masqueraded as the alfresco this café advertised, and swearing on all that was holy to never find myself on her wrong side.

'You're looking nice today, Rune,' I began tentatively, noticing her sandals were colour coordinated to the T-shirt she was wearing. There was no make-up on her face. Not a smidgeon.

For all I knew of Runa from the time I knew her, which was over three decades now, she had had no sex life. Or if she had one, she kept it pretty well hidden. Everything and everyone has sex lives, except for Runa, and of course my parents—I am obviously the result of immaculate conception. Sometimes I think even my shoes have a rabid sex life when the drawers are shut. I'm sure they get busy mating and producing offspring so when I open my drawer, peeking up cheekily at me are all kinds of shoes I have never ever before set eyes on in my entire life, leave alone paid good money for. So obviously space quickly runs out, and I have to use stealth and deception to encroach on drawers occupied by shoes which the spouse doesn't ever remember he has, bundle his into the loft in big plastic bags and shift my spill-over to his drawer. And then act innocent when the spouse suddenly remembers his pair of Versace slip-ons and starts hunting high and low for them.

'Kay, weren't there some of my shoes here?' he asks, puzzled frown creasing handsome forehead.

'How do I know where your shoes are, you should take care of your things,' I answer back and make a grand exit in full theatrical fashion from the room before light dawns in his confused brain. And while he is out, I stealthily take said pair from loft and push them into existing drawer filled with his shoes, and say, 'There, there they are, the shoes you were searching for yesterday. You don't look for things properly, there it will be, right under your nose, but will you see them? No. I will have to come search for them. I wonder how you get things done in the office. . . .' And more in that vein until the poor confused man swears he needs an eye check-up.

To come back to Runa and her opinion on make-up, which I do not share with her, given that I would rather be caught dead in public instead of being seen without lipstick. Why do men not use make-up, she had thundered, slamming her sizeable palm into the thin metal table under the patio umbrella we were sitting at, warming to her favourite theme, while I pondered how any amount of artificial colouring on her face, no matter how skilfully applied, would do nothing to deter from how intimidating she is.

'Er, Runa,' I butted in, before she actually dented the table. I am brave. I rush in where angels keep their distance. 'Men these days wear make-up too. They go to parlours and get every beauty treatment possible done. In fact, the last time I went in for a facial, there were more men than women in the salon.' She raised one sardonic eyebrow—which, I noticed, needed threading. I didn't dare point that out, though. I value my life. I have a small child who depends on me to have a happy childhood and a balanced diet, with nutrition that doesn't come out of packs and taste like salted compressed cardboard.

Which reminded me, I was long overdue on my bi-monthly glycolic peel; my skin was beginning to look like the surface of the moon with appropriate craters. And the lines along the naso labial fold needed serious looking into, preferably including tender ministrations with a syringe depositing a filler. I was so letting myself fall to pieces. I mourned the loss of skin that bounced back into shape after a smile, instead of letting said smile linger on long after the joy of the moment had passed.

I looked at Runa. Sturdy as a tree trunk with visible facial hair. And not a smidgeon of lipstick or gloss. I admired her, her complete unselfconsciousness. And maybe the butch look got her the attention she was looking for. I suddenly felt my gut twist up. I hope we were not looking like what I thought we were looking. I looked around nervously. Surely I looked like a happily married woman. Enough about shallow things like appearances, there were more pressing tasks at hand, including a murder that didn't seem to have been solved.

'Runa,' I said. 'There has been a murder in my complex. Actually two, both outside on the road behind my complex. But one of the victims was a resident of our complex.'

She leaned forward with interest. Even in school, Runa was the one who read the murder mysteries while we contented ourselves with florid romances where the tall, dark and mysterious stranger gave the vapid heroine major angst before consenting to kiss her enough to make her insides melt and her heart beat so rapidly she would have an angina attack. A kiss that would be described over three pages, by which time *we* would be having angina attacks wondering if the action was going to get any hotter, or whether this book could be safely consigned to the dustbin rather than fervent handing around with relevant pages indexed in pencil right up front, with aforementioned passages containing action underlined with trembling hands for the benefit of those who wanted to read up without having to go through the entire book. We were a kindly lot.

'I've read about it, tell me all you know,' she replied. Her ears, if they had been dog ears, would have been standing at attention. Her nose was already sniffing out clues. I looked around, suddenly wondering why I was here, trying to make sense of this murder, and the other, when of course the police was doing their job. I concluded I was a busy bee, with nothing better to do. Plus a dead person was trying to tell me something I couldn't quite understand.

I filled her in as quickly as I could with all the details I knew of the case, adding the strange behaviour of Mr Jaiswal when we had landed up en masse to offer our condolences. I wondered if I should mention that I had been imagining I could see the dead lady. Runa was a practical, non-believing, non-spiritual type. She might just bop me on the head. Or brandish that khukri. I took the risk nonetheless. 'Runa, I think I keep seeing the dead lady. I don't know if I'm losing my mind. I thought I saw her standing in my balcony one night at around three in the morning. The next day, I thought I saw her standing in her balcony looking down at me while I jogged. I saw her husband standing in the balcony with a woman, and the next moment when I looked back up, I saw Sheetal there. Can you make sense of this?' I asked, embarrassed to note that my voice had taken on a pleading, grovelling kind of tone that did not suit my personality.

She looked at me with scorn, as befits one who claims to be seeing netherworldly apparitions. 'Kay, there's no such thing as ghosts. You're probably hallucinating. You were always this, err, high-strung kind. But, this sounds so cut-and-dried a mugging that it doesn't make sense,' she said. A niggling thought that had been troubling me too. 'And the body that you and hubby came across in the middle of the road had a bullet put through its head. This woman had her throat slit. The modus operandi is different. The cases might not be related. Murderers,' she whispered to me, in a mock stage whisper that I was sure carried to the furthest corner of the coffee shop, including the spot behind the pillar, where a couple was holding hands and groping each other, 'generally stick to the same modus operandi, and there is usually a connection between the victims.'

Runa pulled out a notebook and pen from her rucksack and started jotting down points in excited haphazard manner. I looked around the café in stray desultorily manner to check if there were any familiar faces I should be greeting or air-kissing or waving at dependent on the level of acquaintance. No familiar faces, except for an earnest, vest-wearing person sitting in the dim recesses of the coffee shop, looking directly at me. And then smiling, and winking. Bleddy hell, what was Velvet Smoking Jacket Man doing here? And what was protocol to greet a face you didn't know except on winking terms? I nodded my head, in what I hoped was a stately, dignified manner, and turned back to Runa, still busy writing in that scrawly handwriting I remembered from school. Her handwriting was the sort that had the teachers tearing their hair out and assigning marks at random because it was so undecipherable and they didn't dare admit to her that they couldn't understand it.

'Who is hiring me for this one?' she asked suddenly. Ah, the filthy topic of money. Such things should not even be discussed between old school friends, but these are cruel times, and bills have to be paid, and I would have to be straight up and tell Runa no one was footing this bill. Me? I would rather hit the sales. I was clear, and precise. 'I can take you to lunch Runa, that's the best I can offer.' Knowing Runa's appetite as I did, it was a very generous offer. I watched her shovel down her chicken tikka sandwich and marble cake in a couple of bites and marvelled at her ability to not care about the mayo smeared grimly on her upper lip and threatening to fall onto her T-shirt.

'Ah well, then, I'll help you work on it, but I'm not going to do any legwork on this one. I'd rather spend my time solving cases for folks who actually pay me,' she said testily. In a tone that was quite unwarranted for, I thought.

I let the tone pass. I don't take offence easily. Not with school friends from whom I've swiped erasers and copied answers. But did she mean for *me* to do the legwork? 'How do I work on it?' I stuttered. This was a completely new twist of events. I was not cut out for blood and gore; I was a delicate, mincing creature who, had I been Victorian, would have to move around with smelling salts in my skirts. 'I can't deal with murderers and stuff, I can't handle criminals, Runa. Remember Sports Day?' I said, referring to the day when we were in Class V and we'd found ourselves confronted by strange man brandishing flaccid male organ at us frightened little girls trying to find us a ladies cloakroom. And while all the girls fled in fright, I stood rooted to the spot and kept squealing so loudly that Flasher Man stepped back in terror while trying to tell me to hush up with anxious gestures, so he didn't realise he was on a step, toppled over, broke his leg and was hauled off by the security and was soundly thrashed by all and sundry. I think that might have cured him permanently of his urge to display himself to little girls.

'Yes, Squealie,' she replied. So she remembered the nickname I'd got from that incident. 'I remember Sports Day. But you're just going to have to stop being Squealie, aren't you, if you want to get to the bottom of this one?' She hefted her rucksack up and stared at me intently. 'Ask around. Ask the neighbours about the lady who was killed. Ask the security guards of her building. Ask her maids. If you spot the cops who came to meet you, ask them about progress in the case. Go to where she was found, look around, see if there is something you can find.' Unlikely, given that many days had passed since the corpse had been hauled off to the mortuary, but these seemed do-able and I nodded my head vigorously. 'Call me. Tell me whatever you can find out. I am going to snoop around with my contacts,' she said, standing up.

The meeting was at a close. As I got up as well, Velvet Smoking Jacket raised a hand in a casual wave and I was compelled to respond with a wave in return. 'Who's that weird chappie?' asked Runa. 'He looks too sleek to be a guy who fancies you.' I bristled at the implication, but kept silent and mysterious, because I had nothing to say. Being on the wrong side of thirty didn't make one naturally unfanciable, did it?

And then, because I was trying so hard to seem glamorous and mysterious, I couldn't resist shooting myself in the foot. 'Someone I met at a party where I also met Suhaan Khan.' Well, *meeting* Suhaan Khan would be stretching the truth a bit, but we were in the same room, weren't we? Within a yard's distance if you ignored the bodyguards.

She looked at me like I was a specimen of supremely aromatic dog turd she had just scraped off her shoe. 'Suhaan Khan beats up his girlfriends. He's a vile piece of work.' On that pleasant note, we parted ways, Runa promising to do some digging on both cases through her sources in the police department. She stated that she needed to get her hands on the panchnamas. Whatever that may be. She also wanted to find out who the investigating officer on these cases was and have a brief chat with said person to find out the current status of the inquiry, which was surely in process. I did mention Sweaty and Swarthy, but for the life of me couldn't remember their names and had to leave it at that. I offered to have the spouse recollect said names for me, but she gave me a pitiful glance and asked me to do her a favour and go home.

I shimmered away into the afternoon, with murder on my mind. And a very disturbed mind it was. I am a kind-hearted sensitive soul. I take stray cockroaches from my home and let them loose in the balcony, hoping they find other homes to inhabit, favourable wind conditions permitting. Before they hit the asphalt. It is not in my nature to splat them with a slipper. Murder and violence of any sort disturbs me. I cannot watch news bulletins without tears trickling down my face, and if by some chance of fate I land on a documentary on starving children, the world is guaranteed a full-fledged howling session.

So it was with a very disturbed mind that I set about trying to piece the murders together. I pulled out the stack of newspapers collected neatly in a corner for the raddiwalla to remind myself of the details of victim number two. Small-time actor, part-time gigolo, Rohit Sharma had done some bit roles in serials as well as the occasional ad. He was a good-looker, I could see from the photographs that accompanied the articles. His family was based up north and had arrived to claim his body. He'd lived in a rented place in Lokhandwala, and was currently on the verge of signing a big film project. Weren't they all?

Somehow, even though his was the body I'd seen, his death didn't fascinate me as much as Sheetal Jaiswal's did. Perhaps because it was her wraith spooking me out every single day. It was almost like she was trying to communicate something to me. I had no clue, though, why she'd chosen me of all people. Perhaps I needed to get in touch with a psychic who could interpret the visitations for me. Or maybe I was hallucinating and needed a psychiatrist instead?

Exhausted by all the reading, I got up and reached deep into the inner recesses of the freezer. A tub of full fat chocolate almond ice cream was calling out my name from inside its deep cool confines. I spooned all its contents into my throat and felt the full fat molecules zip through my bloodstream and decide on where within my epidermis they wanted to take up permanent residency. There is something acutely comforting about having fat ingested in a mindless fashion. It clouds your brain with a pleasant, feel-good haze. You sit, having pigged out to your heart's content, ready to take on the world and Medusas and Aegean stables and Minotaurs in mazes and the cleaning of the wardrobe, till you realise you don't have the get up and go to clean the sink. So you lean back, pick up a copy of a fashion magazine, and pore over the photographs and sigh in sheer want. Ever read that report about why women would rather shop than have sex? No? I recommend you do. And once you've let the woman shop, she will Want You Right Now.

Back to the corpses who were occupying much of my limited cranial space. I didn't have much to go on at this point. Perhaps I needed to pay Sweaty and Swarthy a visit. I debated, and then decided to call Raji on the intercom. Raji was the font of all information of goings-on in the society. Sometimes I suspected that Raji had a hidden room aka William Baldwin in *Sliver*, where she monitored everyone's lives. I once voiced this concern to her, to be greeted with braying dismissive laughter which encouraged me to drop the idea. Nonetheless, Raji was the woman to turn to in the building when all sources of information dried up.

'Hey, any clue about whether they've solved Sheetal's murder?'

Raji was not pleased about being woken from her afternoon siesta to discuss the murder of someone whose husband had not even invited us into his house when we'd visited. Raji is a big one for being invited into homes so she can check out the décor and make notes if she finds anything interesting. 'Her husband was so ungracious,' she said in similar graceless manner herself.

It seemed rather unfair to tie a woman's life to her husband's graciousness or lack of it, I informed her. I added for fair measure that I was sure the spouse would be equally ungracious if I were found with a slit in my thorax on a deserted road, especially when confronted with what seemed like a mini army of women clad in whites, none of whom he knew. 'He's grieving, the poor man. Have a heart, Raji, he probably didn't want to burst into tears in front of a dozen strange women.'

That made sense to her. She grunted and said she didn't know if there'd been any headway in finding the murderer. 'But I do know that there is some woman who keeps visiting, I see her in the balcony sometimes . . .' she added. She had the advantage of a direct view, her balcony being parallel to Sheetal Jaiswal's, albeit a couple of buildings away. 'Could be a relative,' she mulled. 'Could be a sister who visits or something to ensure he's eating and not grieving away to skin and bone. Anyway, are you coming to Kavya's birthday party this evening? Please come, I will die of boredom if I am the only mom around.'

One of the perils of living in such mammoth residential complexes swarming with children of every age and denomination meant that one attended an average of two birthday parties a week, on a regular basis. We had now become birthday party veterans—'we' being the paranoid category of mothers who would not depute birthday party supervision to the maids, and insist on accompanying the spawn of our wombs to ensure they didn't get into more serious mischief than bursting balloons or the occasional fisticuffs in which nothing but the ego would be bruised.

I agreed to go, for the sake of the case. Surely other residents would be in attendance, supervising their kids. And the clubhouse was right at the back of the complex. Near the turn-off where Sheetal had been found, and barely ten yards from where the poor sod with the bullet through his brain had been dumped. I planned to walk around the spots and look for clues. I was rather chuffed at the thought of looking for clues. I felt like Miss Marple, save the quick-thinking and the detective skills, and of course the white hair. I practiced a mysterious Miss Marple smile. I wondered if I should take magnifying glass and plastic Ziploc bags along with me. What did detectives carry with them? How did one play detective detective? I had no knowledge of forensics, nor ballistics, and I didn't have a degree in psychology that would help me make conclusions about motive and such like relevant things. It was all so beyond anything I had ever done before, that I thought it best to just stroll down to the scene of the crime and look around the jetsam and flotsam undoubtedly lying around on the road. Naturally, a lot would have already been scoured up by the forensics team of the police department. But one never knew.

My reverie was interrupted by the child squawking violently about his complete lack of interest in attending a girl's birthday party. 'Dere wil be Barbie dolls everywhere!!' he spat out in vitriolic disgust. 'I is nod going for a gurl's budday pahty. All my frens will laffatme.'

I mentioned the wonderful, irresistible prospect of a return gift and unlimited cake, and his mind quickly jumped onto the fence. 'Bud, I'll aks the antie fer d redurngeef when I go inside, fusht oney. And the cake. And we will come home fast before my frens see me.'

I assured him that this would be alright, thinking, 'Fast forward twenty years and I bet you'll write away half your inheritance, plus your parents' false teeth to be the only male at an all-girl party.'

'An don make me sid wid Kavya or her stoopid frens okay,' he instructed me sternly as I spit polished him in waistcoat and striped shirt, into party mode. 'And I don wantu eat d stoopid Barbie cake!' he spat out as a final warning.

I slipped into a fresh pair of jeans and a pale peach chiffon kurti with slight sequin work at the neck and cuffs; it wasn't day wear, nor full-fledged evening wear either, but just right for the kind of in-between occasions that kiddy birthday parties were. The shoes were debated on: should I go with flat gold thongs, or matte metallic kitten heels. I settled for the thongs. I had walking to do. And some on-the-spot investigations. And I didn't think kitten heels would allow any walking around without click-clacking my arrival to the world and stray lurking muggers. Not that there would be muggers lurking around on a bright winter evening like this, when the sun was dipping gently over the horizon and the air was redolent with the voices of those playing their game of tennis or splashing in the pool. But one could never be too careful, and I put the can of pepper spray back into my bag, resolving to check the visage of the attacker before spraying into it, if the need arose again. I trotted over to my drawer with the ready wrapped stock of birthday gifts I keep and pulled out a girl-appropriate one.

The party was already in progress by the time we reached. Raji and a couple of other moms had draped themselves languidly in chairs on the fringes of the party hall, which strangely enough opened right onto the poolside, which was great if one wanted to host a nice dinner for grown-ups, but not ideal for a party with lots of kids, and kids on sugar too. As it is, Raji and the other moms were doing their best to watch the swinging doors into which the children were running into with amazing clockwork regularity.

I deposited the child in their custody, getting them to swear on all that was holy that they would ensure he didn't step a foot outside the swinging glass doors, and took myself off to the spot I had been told was where Sheetal Jaiswal had been found.

I stood there and looked around vacantly, trying to piece the moment together. Reconstructing the crime scene, in detective speak. I had re-read a couple of crime novels, or rather skim-read them. Like I do most books that don't really interest me. But hush, let's not tell anyone about that now, okay.

I came in from the spot Sheetal must have jogged in from. The late evening sun hit my eyes at a slant, and I quickly slammed on my Tom Ford Samantha Bug Eyes. And felt the world a much more manageable haze of biscuit brown. The angle of the slash across the neck, said the forensic expert quoted in the newspapers, indicated the attack was from behind. Sneaky that. No moral courage to confront the victim and then attack. I looked around at the spot where she would have fallen. Of course, the ground would have been dusted of all forensic evidence. I wouldn't even know what constituted forensic evidence. Nonetheless, I looked around. I knew that her iPod was found lying a little away from her body. Of the jewellery on her body, only her chain had been removed, that much I had heard from the grapevine and read in the newspapers. And then there was the issue of her shoes.

Only a dull stain on the asphalt indicated what must have been a pool of blood. I walked slowly up and down the road; there was no pavement here, just rows of bushes planted hastily along the side of the asphalt struggling to rise asthmatically above the ground. The road, sleek and shining with the reflected sun, was recently built over reclaimed marsh land. Smooth, and unlined. Ah, well, not quite so smooth, a few cracks here and there, and one rather huge one that I almost tripped over, looked back and spewed some violent words at.

Something caught my eye, as I was looking balefully at said crack. Something almost covered with the mud and stones. I bent down, pulling my trousers up so they wouldn't touch the road and gain mud stains, and looked hard. Maybe I should have put in my eye-lubricating drops before I had set out on this expedition. I broke a twig off the nearest bush and pushed the mud and gravel aside to find the glint of something ornamental.

I bent down to pick it up. With my eyebrow tweezers of course; I wouldn't dare risk putting fingers to anything remotely suspicious. Yes of course I carry my eyebrow tweezers in my bag, never know when one might spot an errant strand waving cheekily at one.

The glinting object was a pendant. A pendant with Ma Sherawali sitting serenely on her tiger, fringed with diamantes. The type handed over to you if you attended the Mata Ki Chowkis held with religious zeal in almost every complex to which all and sundry were invited. Where had I read that Sheetal Jaiswal had worn a pendant with no value, which had gone missing along with the gold chain? This pendant had a couple of diamantes missing. Maybe they had fallen off in the grapple for the now-missing chain. I don't think Sheetal Jaiswal, being as particular about coordinated scrunchies as she was, would wear a pendant with missing diamantes, even if it *was* religious.

I popped it into one the Ziploc pouches I'd finally decided to carry along. I continued to look around but saw nothing of note except the apologetic shrubbery. As I turned back to the clubhouse, I spotted, snagged on branches, a familiar pink hair band, now faded and dirty. But familiar. I did a little jump in the air and looked around guiltily to check if anyone had noticed. I could feel my heart thudding with excitement in my chest. Surely there would be evidence of some kind on this too, which could help the cops. I extricated it gently from the branches with a handkerchief and put it into another Ziploc bag. I was getting good at this detective business, I thought happily. I could make this a vocation. I would be called on by the police to assist them in their investigations. But first, I needed to let the boss know.

I messaged Runa that I had found two things at the crime scene which I wanted to hand over to her. I thought they could be evidence, I added chirpily. But when I returned to the party, where the boys had by now happily made Wolverine fists with toothpicks and were attacking the balloons, I wondered if what I had found really *was* of any consequence to the investigation. Had the forensic experts and the police constables and inspectors hovering around missed these things altogether?

The very harried games host called out weakly to the boys to come together for yet another exciting game of statue or passing the parcel or musical chairs, to which they snorted in his face scornfully and continued their trail of destruction and mayhem. The girls stood bunched in corners and meekly obeyed the games host, with an occasional couple of tomboys crossing over to the boys' side of the divide and joining the fun.

We staggered home a couple of hours later where I downed a couple of aspirins with stiff gin and tonic to keep the migraines at bay and the child continued to shoot pellets from the mini Glock he'd got as his return gift. I confiscated the gift when one pellet decided to attack my eye, making the eyelid swell up to hooded crook levels. Strangely no one seemed to notice too much of a difference in my face, and I wondered aloud if everyone had simultaneously developed a need for spectacles. I iced my eye, sipped my gin and tucked the fake Glock into my handbag. It would come in handy if I were ever confronted by a mugger, or worse, a man with a knife intent on slitting my throat.

# CHAPTER 9

# IN WHICH MANY QUESTIONS ARE ASKED

THE NEXT MORNING DAWNED BRIGHT and clear. In fact, so terribly bright and clear, that my eyes hurt as I jogged determinedly on the track at 6.30 a.m.

Jogging on the track made me gain newfound sympathy for animals in cages, condemned to pace up and down and circle the small enclosures they were summarily dumped in for visitors to gawp at. I felt like an animal in a cage, if animals in cages could wear brown velour track pants and matching hoodies over a lycra vest.

I did my hour-long routine and returned home wondering why it was that Runa had not seemed as elated as I had been with my discovery. All she'd said to the SMS I had sent was a noncommittal, 'Okay'. Was this the end of my career as a desi Miss Marple, even before it began? I put such questions to the back of my brain, which wasn't a difficult task to do, and concentrated on the morning routine.

The cook and Jamuna were bickering again in the kitchen, with Jamuna tossing insulting asides about the lack of culinary skills possessed by the cook in her native tongue, to which the cook, furious but unable to respond in same tongue, was retorting by slamming utensils around at startling intervals, making me jump out of my skin on more than one occasion in a thirty-minute span. I kept checking my phone obsessively in case Runa had messaged or called and I had missed it, and the two Ziploc pouches lay heavy in my bag and on my heart, with me wondering what I was supposed to do with them. Nada. Nothing from Runa.

I sighed. Deeply. As deeply as it was possible to sigh without getting oxygen-deprived and lightheaded. I called up Raji on the intercom to check if she had unearthed any more gossip from her stint as the keeper of the swinging doors at the birthday party yesterday. Nada, she said. 'But I heard that Debina of 1202 is having an affair with her gym instructor. Confirmed news. She was spotted having coffee with him at the Barista across the road.'

I rubbished her conclusion stating that a couple having an affair would hardly choose to meet up in full view of the entire paying public from the complex, but she was not convinced.

The child and the spouse were packed off to school and office respectively, with all relevant and appropriate tiffin and lunch boxes accompanying the right person.

I tackled my daily phone call to the parents, wherein I made tentative plans of visiting them over the forthcoming Christmas holidays, and the pater promised to check their social calendar to revert as to which days were relatively free for them to entertain us.

The father, you see, is a member of everything he could possibly be a member of, from the local reading and laughter clubs to the local NGO teaching street kids to read and write and not get into fistfights. 'I think post Christmas would be better,' he intoned thoughtfully. 'We have just too much scheduled around Christmas time, and then we leave for our trip to Bandhavgarh in the first week of January. We're going to stay in tents.' Have I mentioned that the father is also a wildlife enthusiast? Given a choice between spending time with his grandson and chasing a tiger's spoor in a wildlife sanctuary, the latter would win hands down. Of course, he would share the prized photographs, edited, labelled and compiled into a slideshow with the child who would sit and watch till his eyes glazed over.

I could just visualise the mater, sitting uneasily in a tent, jumping out of her skin at every suspicious sound from the darkness. 'At this age, he wants me to rough it out,' she complained bitterly, when the line was passed on to her. 'I didn't rough it out in my parents' home. I had servants who brought me water in a glass . . .' The pater grumbled amiably in the background about her being welcome to return to her parents' home whenever she desired and the topic was changed.

'Come anytime you want, darling,' said the mater, threatening to hop onto an intercity bus herself and come visit, and would have done so if she hadn't been so worried about the pater, who insisted on doing obscene things to his glucose levels by sneaking in forbidden foods when the mother turned her back.

'It is all safe at your side, na, Kananbeta,' she asked, with a frown creasing her voice. 'I hope you're not being stupid and going jogging at early hours.' Err. I was not about to confess publicly about my stupidity, but then it seemed to be one of the foregone conclusions with anyone who interacted with me, so I let the slur on my grey cells pass undebated. She grumbled for the standard five minutes more about my only sibling and his current plans of retiring as a bachelor and dying of old age, alone and unmourned in a foreign land, begging me to talk sense into him and tell him to settle down with a good girl, good being an amorphous blend of someone who could pub hop with him and take them on pilgrimages without needing to be a case of split personality.

Post conversation, I plan out my day, if it hasn't been planned out already the previous day. If the day lies empty, with no lunches, movies or shopping trips planned with the girls, I devote it to domesticity. And that is what today looked to be drifting towards. The pleasures of vegetable shopping. And grocery shopping.

I showered, changed into a pair of capris and a shift top in a blazing canary yellow which echoed the sunlight outside. Pulled all my hair into a tight ponytail, perfect for fighting the throngs in the supermarket, and stuck on my big pair of sunnies over my eyes. What? You honestly didn't think I go to a vegetable market, risk slipping on slushy rotting vegetable refuse lining the road, and then bend over and haggle with the vendors? Over my dead body. I am that statistic of the urban-educated housewife who wants convenience and pre-packaged vegetables at her local supermarket, and whose idea of grocery shopping is a large trolley filled to bursting capacity once every couple of weeks. I want to pick from a display of fresh produce, all washed, cleaned, packed carefully into plastic packets with holes punched into them, without having to wonder whether the vendor is making his equivalent of a killing on the price he is quoting, looking around in a mini panic to ask the seemingly more experienced matrons around what I should actually pay because the rate quoted seems to include the price of gold and platinum at current market prices. No, the uncertainty would kill me. I'd rather pick up all my veggies in five minutes flat and breathe a sigh of relief and not worry whether the sabziwallah got his weekly quota of eye-popping sights when I bent down to pick and sort the veggies.

So there I was, nudging my trolley inch by inch down the crowded aisle when someone said a bright and cheery hello from behind me. It was a voice that was hovering on the borderline between familiar and unfamiliar. I turned round with a start. It was the Velvet Smoking Jacket. Today clad in a regular pair of jeans and a rather ugly black T-shirt with a snake crawling through the eye sockets of a skull that had a rose strategically placed between its teeth—a T-shirt I was sure would cost me the equivalent of a hair-rebonding session. I'm sure there was a carpe diem message here from Andrew Marvell that I couldn't quite get the subliminal implications of.

'The veggies any good here?' he asked, with the kind of grin that would make any right-thinking, hormonally-driven woman keel over, die and go to a heaven which is populated by muscular, shaved men in thongs. I am not hormonally driven. It has been a while since I have been hormonally driven. I almost sputtered what are you doing here, and realised I had. And it had sounded just as rude as it did in my head.

'I've half moved into the complex right behind,' he said gravely. 'I'll probably shop here from now on.'

I had a sudden coughing fit, which ended with him gallantly taking a bottle of mineral water from the display and offering it to me. 'Oh,' I replied in a small, uncertain voice, 'welcome. I live there too.'

He raised one sardonic eyebrow. 'Oh, this move will be more fun than I'd expected.'

I felt my face turning the ugly beetroot red it does in total traitor-like fashion whenever I am embarrassed. This is not the way a soigné woman of the world behaves. A soigné woman of the world would raise an eyebrow right back and say something immensely witty right back to the lines of, 'Well, we would just have to find out, wouldn't we?'

Me, I sputtered the water I was drinking right back out, making a royal mess of the canary yellow frontage of my shift top, and made a quick exit, throwing whatever vegetables I could lay my hands on into my trolley and rushing out to the check-out queue.

'You'll have to get them to bill that bottle of water,' he yelled out at my retreating behind.

As I waited for the driver to load the contents of the trolley into the car, my phone rang. Or Robbie Williams sang *She's the One*. What? What? I love Robbie Williams. I love his ballads. I am of the soppy generation who grew up on Air Supply. If you remember them, gentle reader, two gentlemen belting out soulful romantic numbers designed to twist your gut into mush and make you run out shrieking and mug the first available male in your path with Valentine's Day cards. Songs designed to make you look soppily at the pimply, gangly cretin next door who kept his mouth open like a goldfish whenever you pass. Songs that most respectable people now seem to have developed a collective amnesia for, given that we have more exciting things like Lady Gaga and Rihanna, and Akon and songs by them hip hop artistes that speak of stuff which could have probably got you arrested for public indecency and instigating violence back in my day.

I looked at the screen to find Runa screaming at me in capital letters. Much like she would in person. 'Pick the damn phone Kay,' I could almost hear her.

'Yes, Runa,' I answered. 'Where are you?' My tone, I suspected, a trifle whiny.

'I am right here, darling, where are you? I trotted all the way down to your neck of the woods to find you AWOL. Aren't you supposed to be playing housewife or something, and be dusting the potted plants?'

I tried hard not to take offence, even though, truth be told, I do spray each leaf to keep the dust off every other day. It's a dusty place we live in, what with the never-ending construction sending across tonnes of dust molecules designated to settle down and multiply on my plants, sofas and every available surface. And leaves do get dusty so easily, don't they?

'Where are you now?' I asked peevishly, refusing to discuss my whereabouts, or reveal I have been doing hopelessly domesticated tasks like grocery shopping.

'I'm in the lobby of your building. I've already finished chatting up two of your watchmen and I am now going across to the building where the dead body lived,' she answered like a woman with a plan.

Dead Body? That sounded so dehumanising. She had been a person, a flesh-and-blood person, with a rude husband and a persistent weight problem. And the ignominy of an unpleasant death at the hands of a random thief. I felt sorry for her. 'Her name was Sheetal, Runa,' I said softly. 'Don't call her Dead Body.' I could almost feel Runa raise one stern, unthreaded eyebrow.

'Sure. Sheetal. Now I want to have a look at the trinket you found on the road. I've already checked out the spot—the security rounder was kind enough to take me there. And I've met the investigating officer on the case. He wasn't very helpful, but he did show me the findings of the investigation and the postmortem report. Come back quick, I've got Mr Rathore here with me to help us out.'

I had scary visions of Runa hauling our diminutive security rounder by the collar and frogmarching him to the end of the road. 'I'll be there in five minutes,' I replied with as much authority as I could muster.

It is something that never fails to amaze me. With some people who've known me from the time I was a pimple-encrusted, bespectacled, braces-afflicted prepubescent, I automatically regress to the whiny, defensive kid I was, with no comeback line when she needs one. Runa was one of those people who immediately got me into the apologising-for-my-presence-on-this-planet kind of frame of mind. You know the feeling? Do you have anyone in your life who makes you feel the same way? Shall we take out a joint contract on their lives and avail of group discounts on the same? Ah well, you know what I mean.

I rushed in a sullen mood to the complex premises where, true to form, my first sight was Runa, towering over the security rounder, looking to all purposes like a grim Severus Snape giving a thirteen-year-old Harry Potter a good ticking off plus detention, plus points taken away from Gryffindor. She looked up at me as I entered and winked cheekily. I was almost thrown off balance. Runa winking cheekily was like seeing the Queen Mother do a burlesque dance. Totally out of character, and enough to make my jaw drop.

'Kay!' she bore down upon me with the kind of bonhomie I was sure she reserved for professional purposes, since she had never ever employed it on a personal level for all the decades I had known her. 'This kind gentleman here, Mr Rathore, has been immensely helpful to my investigation.'

Mr Rathore looked like a deer caught in the headlights of an oncoming truck, and blinked rapidly, if deer caught in headlights do indeed blink rapidly.

'And just one final thing Mr Rathore, I would just like to know if you have seen anyone wearing this before?' She held out her hand to me and hissed in my ear in a style more suitable to the Runa I knew from days of yore, 'Give me the pendant, Kay . . .' I quickly dug out the Ziploc pouch and handed it to her.

Rathore stared at it with his eyes getting more deer-in-the-headlight-like. 'No Madam,' he said with a deferential air, which puzzled me. On every occasion I have had the opportunity of interacting with him, Rathore has behaved more like a deranged rodent with rabid slavering jaws, ready to attack.

'I cannot remember if I have seen it before, but let us ask the other security staff,' he replied in a manner so mild and meek, I would have fainted with shock had anyone else reported such meekness on his part to me. I had to hold onto the granite-encased walls to prop myself up. Too many minor shocks in the past hour. Cheeky Velvet Smoking Jacket moving into our residential complex. Frothing at the mouth Mr Rathore behaving like the lion who lay down with the lamb. It was too much for my weak heart to take.

He blew a whistle and the security men scurried to line up in front of him, 'Yeh madam ke haath mein jo pendant hai, isko theek se dekho aur socho, kya tumne kissi ko isse pehene huye dekha hai?'

The security guards circled Runa obediently and looked at the pendant through the Ziploc pouch she was holding up. They all shook their heads in the negative and filed back to their positions wordlessly, waiting for the next command.

Runa pocketed the Ziploc and smiled fondly at Rathore like a lady might at her newly-acquired puppy who has just learnt that no, the leg of the sofa is not where your business should be done, no. I half expected her to say 'Good boy' and ruffle his hair. I think she restrained herself with tremendous self control. She looked down on him and shook his hand vigorously. 'Rathore saab you were a great help to me. Thank you so much.'

He looked up and beamed. 'Anytime Madam, if I can be of any help do tell me.'

'How did you get him to be so helpful?' I hissed as we moved away towards the gate.

'I showed him my fake CBI card,' she hissed back.

I froze in shock. This was against the law. She could get arrested and get me arrested in the process for being her accomplice.

Runa marched on like a woman with a plan. I am wary of women with plans. Especially women who have very random plans and expect me to follow their plans. 'Where are you going now?' I asked her.

'I went to Sheetal's flat, but no one seemed to be at home, so I'm off to check the spot where she was found,' she gestured expansively, almost knocking my sunglasses off my face. I pushed them back into position in a swift alert response that made me rather proud of my reflexes.

'It's too hot to go traipsing all over the place,' I said, summoning my car with an imperious wave.

'I would rather walk around the place,' Runa replied. 'It gives me a feel for the crime scene.'

'But you already saw the crime scene, didn't you?' I whined, regressing promptly to the fat, pimply, twelve-year-old with self-esteem issues.

She marched on purposefully, leaving me no choice but to follow. 'Runa, I have to get back; the child's school bus will be here in half an hour,' I said in the same whiny tone.

She relented and hopped into the car. We drove down to where sandwich-wallahs and cutting-chai wallahs littered the side of the road with the refuse of their produce. Runa asked one of them randomly if he was around on the night when the dead body was found on the back road. Very much so, he answered. Did he see anything unusual that day, she asked. Nothing. So had we reached a dead end? I was already bored of this detective business. It was hot and I was sweaty and involved in chatting up watchmen and sandwich-wallahs. Where was the glamour? Where was the drama? Where was the glory?

I wanted to hand in my resignation. I suggested as much to Runa. 'Let's stop trying to interfere in police work; after all, we don't have to do this . . .'

She stared at me with her beady eyes, which was rather like being impaled under the red eye of pain belonging to Jane the Volturi. I squirmed and jumped out of its path. 'I'm having fun now,' she replied. 'Plus I have no cases on hand right now, and I need to stay in practice.'

I gritted my teeth and followed her. I fished out my Neutrogena Ultra Sheer Helioplex SPF 50 sunblock from the deep recesses of my fake Bottega Veneta Intrecciato and applied it liberally, oblivious to the perplexed and openly-amused glances I got from onlookers munching into their veg sandwiches, sipping their cutting chais. What? What? What? I have skin that tans easily and I do not rock the bronzed look. No sir.

I fished about some more in the bag and pulled on my visor. I need a visor. Even with the sunglasses. You need to stop the wrinkles from happening. And the sun is the biggest wrinkle-inducer. You see those horrific ads about how the sunrays hit your skin through glass, through cloudy weather . . . oh you mean they have a product to sell? Doesn't matter, I'm taking no chances; there are spidery lines fanning out from the edge of my eyes, which give me a perpetual squinting-against-the-sun kind of a look. This would look interesting if I had been a portrait in the *National Geographic,* but since I'm not, I spend five minutes patting down the area with an eye cream every night with the ring finger of my right hand—pat not rub, mind you—before I can doze off in peace.

We took the car to the back road where the spouse and I had almost driven over Mr Bullet Hole in Head. 'I have a copy of the forensics report,' Runa stated blandly, leading me to have newfound admiration for her investigative skills. 'The weapon has been identified, and is being tracked down. This case is has no connection to the murder of the lady from your building complex. I think the police will be making arrests on this one by the end of the day.'

My jaw thudded to the concrete, I quickly picked it up and pushed it back into place.

Runa emerged from the car and looked around at the road, which looked back at her, as bland and nondescript as a back road parallel to a creek needed to be. Runa said matter-of-factly that she thought she had some leads, and that we would need to make another visit to the police station to meet the investigating officer on the cases.

'Aaargh,' I moaned. 'I'm not going to meet Sweaty and Swarthy again. Please. I've got to go home. I don't think I'm cut out for detective work. I resign.'

Runa fixed the eye of intense back-bending pain on me again. 'You're gone soft Kay. You're calling it quits even before we start. I didn't expect this from you.'

I nodded petulantly. 'It's bleddy boring. I'm going home now. The child will be back and he will be throwing all sorts of tantrums to ensure he has a lunch of Maggi noodles. And here's the hair band.' I fished out the other Ziploc pouch and handed it to her. I expected the heralding of some trumpets in the background but there was nothing except the sound of the random, toneless honking that goes for music on most urban streets.

She peered at it, shrugged and said, 'Anyway, I'm going to the police station, and I am going to do some asking around at Lokhandwala where the chappie who was killed lived. If I do find out anything of consequence, I will let you know. And Kay,' she said in a resigned tone that was very hurtful to my ego, 'Ask around, will you?'

And she stomped off with her pound-the-earth walk that made no concessions to femininity at all. It was the kind of walk that the Amazons, had they still been around ruling their part of the planet, spearing innocent weakling men types, would have walked. It was also the kind of walk that, had I walked it, would have sent the mother into instant spasms of an anxiety attack as to how she would ever find a spouse for such an ungraceful creature.

My mother is big on grace. She has clear and definite ideas of what constitutes feminine behaviour, and this does not include stomping off with a walk that does not guarantee that the road beneath will not quiver from the impact. She also believes that a woman should laugh delicately and despairs of the neighing and snorting I am prone to when I decide that something is funny. The kind of laugh that can be heard in the immediate vicinity by all and sundry, who then cast strange looks at me especially if said laughing occurs in a public situation like a restaurant or a coffee shop, or horror of horror, at a religious function. I have come close to being disinherited on more occasion than one, in situations involving a prayer meeting to mourn for a departed friend/relative/acquaintance and me checking out SMS jokes. I have since learnt that jokes are not appropriate reading matter on such occasions and instead concentrate on my credit card payment reminders; those automatically lengthen my jaw to the ground and make the tears spring forthwith to mine eyes.

Needless to say, I have failed my mother long and often in the graceful department. I do not walk swaying gracefully like a leaf on a branch being gently blown by the wind. I walk determinedly, purposefully and often so lost in my thoughts that I pass my destination and realise I've done so approximately ten minutes too late.

When I landed back home, the child was, true to expectation, rolling on the floor in a petulant demand for Maggi Thrilling Curry wid Maaza, while Jamuna was trying frantically to houri dance in front of him with a plate stacked with the healthy, nutritious stuff.

'Kabir,' I bent down to his ground level, 'get up from the ground. Your clothes will get dirty.'

If there is one thing I know to do with my son, it is that in situations of tantrum-ing, appeal to the dandy in him. It immediately sobers him down. He has, in this sense, taken completely after me. When he goes down to the playground, he needs to be encased in a jacket, full-length jeans and a T-shirt that matches the stitching or the decals on the jeans.

The thought of his clothes getting dirty stopped the rolling on the floor, but he calmly took himself to the bed and continued with said rolling-styled tantrum-ing. 'I wan Maggi Tillin Curry wid Maazaa which is cole frum d fridz. I wantit now. Gimme. Gimme.'

As I do in the sane, sensible and practical way of dealing with unreasonable tantrum-ing, I gave him the Maggi and Maaza, and settled down for an afternoon nap. What? Of course, I nap in the afternoons. Haven't you heard of power-napping? It is what famous and busy people do in order to recharge their batteries and get their brain cells in full firing mode again. It is what we non-famous and non-busy people do as well if we want to feel human in the evenings. I fell into a deep confused sleep where I saw Velvet Smoking Jacket slitting Sheetal Jaiswal's throat, while I worried whether the outfit I was wearing clung too much to my multiple stomachs. And Bristly standing at the edge of the road, puffing on a cigarette and telling me to make him a cup of tea. And me wondering how on earth I was supposed to make a cup of tea in the middle of the road, with no gas stove or tea leaves or utensils in sight. Why was I even making Bristly tea when I bristled to make a cuppa for my beloved spouse? I knew then it was a dream. And woke up to find it was late evening and I had multiple missed calls from Runa on my mobile.

I scrambled up in guilt and called her back. 'Where the eff were you, Kay?' Runa barked on the first ring.

'I was, err, busy,' I replied sheepishly, glad that video technology had not yet become popular in the cellular phone business. 'So tell me, did you find out anything?'

'I met the officers investigating both cases. Kay, they both seem pretty cut-and-dried—they've even arrested the suspects.' My jaw dropped as low as it could without actually clunking on the ground and impacting my molars. 'There seems to be nothing more to be done, so let's close the cases.'

Close the cases? The rush of disappointment surprised me. I felt kind of cheated. You know. You expect to find a case filled with intrigue and evil motives and scheming, and you are handed across a boring murder with none of the above, except simple robbery as a motive. Rather defeats the purpose of life, doesn't it? And then, what about the two pieces of absolutely vital evidence that I had picked off the street, I wanted to ask, but held my peace till she had said her piece. Rune hates to be interrupted. It disturbs her thought process, she says. I let her thought process run on.

'The Sheetal Jaiswal murder was apparently the handiwork of a local junkie who mugged her and killed her in panic when she put up a fight. They've recovered her chain from a local jewellery store. The owner described the fellow as one who regularly came to him to sell stolen stuff. Her husband is going to the police station to identify the pendant you found, which I handed over to the cops.' She paused. 'The guy who murdered her was wearing her shoes when he went to sell the chain. The shoes caught the jeweller's eye, ladies shoes they were. Clearly ladies shoes, and he mentioned it to the police.'

But they had bright pink stripes down the side. Only a brave man would wear those in public. Maybe he was a metrosexual, this murderer chappie. I mean, there were enough and more men wearing colours like baby pink these days and rolling up their sleeves to show biceps. There was really no accounting for taste these days.

'And the other chappie?' I asked sadly, not really interested in what had caused the poor man to end up in the middle of a deserted road on a Friday night with a bullet through his brain, rather than whooping it up at the party for which he was so obviously dressed.

'Ah now,' she simpered gleefully, with as much simpering as she was capable of, 'that's an interesting story. This guy was a male gigolo. Apparently he was blackmailing one of his clients for a role in a movie. Now this client is a big-time movie producer. The police have a theory that he was killed in a contract put out by this producer, and dumped near your complex. But they haven't got a confession in yet.'

I chewed on that news for a bit, and found it a bit gristly and hard to digest. But Runa would have got her facts right. She was efficient at her work; didn't people pay her good money to tackle errant spouses, to dig out phone stalkers and to investigate the real causes of death, especially when property was involved?

'Hmm,' I said.

'Hmm,' I repeated, because I really had nothing to say.

'I would have expected a more animated response than "Hmmm",' Runa said in her granite-cutter voice. 'Especially considering this is an unpaid-for assignment I took on just because you are an old school friend.'

'Hmm,' I replied, her granite-cutter voice not having made a dent into my thoughts. 'Then why did the junkie not take her iPod? He could have sold it too.'

For once, there was silence at the other end of the line.

# CHAPTER 10

# OF A WEEKEND
# SPENT AT A COTTAGE
# MULLING OVER
# GHOSTLY ENCOUNTERS

**T**HE NORMAL MORNING RUN WAS dispensed with the next morning, since we had planned to take off to Lonavla, it being the long Christmas weekend, and the child having begun his Christmas vacations.

Our bags had been packed the previous night. It is a long and arduous task, this bag-packing business. In the good old days when life was young, I was thin, and the child was but a gleam in his father's eye, our packing comprised dumping a couple of sets of clothes into a duffel bag and then taking off at the crack of dawn for cross-country drives with nothing to fortify ourselves except the dhaba food one would pick up along the way. We had iron-clad guts we prided on. Intestines that no bacteria could hope to attack and infect.

With the advent of the child, travelling had changed completely. For one, the need to pack for the child. And as anyone who is a parent knows, a child can be guaranteed to wet, throw up on, dirty, stain and generally muck up more clothes on a single day than you would wear in a week, a score that they manage to accelerate to the speed of light on trips when you have limited clothes packed and no inclination to wash and dry-out things. I still shudder at the memory of a road trip to Goa, where we landed in the lobby of Fort Aguada encrusted with vomit and looking like urchins who had no business being in its hallowed precincts. Needless to say, while the father and son lived it up in the pool, I was saddled with the unenviable task of converting the bathtub into a washtub to clean kiddy puke from all our clothes.

This was before I discovered Avomine, a wonder drug that not only ensures that the child snores throughout the trip, but also stays puke-free. I pack lighter since.

For the child, that is.

Packing for myself is another ball game altogether. I need to pack practical travelling clothes. Practical travelling shoes which are sturdy enough to run around chasing the child around luggage carousels at airports. Then clothes for the day. Clothes for nights out, if any. Formal clothes in case the occasion arises. Like James Bond, I always like to be prepared, with coordinated shoes and handbag. Which gives rise to the need for two to three pairs of shoes. Which in turn gives rise to the need for an additional bag. Which in turn increases the luggage we need to carry. Which then makes the spouse bark about how he hopes I don't plan on him carrying all the luggage while I'm conveniently occupied with the child. Which then ends with me sulking and him deciding to open up the suitcases and gasping at the number of clothes packed within.

'Kay!!! We are going for three days! You have twenty tops and eight trousers! And four skirts. And three pairs of stilettos. Where do you think you will wear stilettos on the mountain roads?'

What if there is a discotheque in the hotel? Men would never understand. Also, I'm one of those who likes to have her options when she is getting dressed in the morning. Unless I have considered and discarded at least four or five ensembles along with coordinated shoes and handbag, I don't feel I have dressed to sufficient impact.

I tend to discard a lot of ensembles because, sadly, I have a dressing table with a three-way mirror, which is the greatest mistake for any right-thinking woman if she must get dressed quickly. For one, you start off by looking at your reflection up front. It seems decent enough, with all the wobbly bits and pieces tucked away carefully. Then you decide to sneak a peek at the reflection from the left. First you are sidewhopped by the protuberance that is your behind. You turn to reach a more satisfying profile and realise that you have the kind of behind that is – as the fashion experts put it—sitar-shaped, and a top that decides to settle at the top of the ledge is so not a great idea. So you change into a top that is empire line and flares out a bit, and will cling to the upper body emphasising the only part about you that is still worth a dekko, and gently camouflage the bits around the waist that decide to march to a different drummer. And you decide to wear this with a pair of tights. You look at yourself looking perfectly svelte and the kind of sexy some strange sod might still find it in his heart to wolf-whistle at, when you spot the mottled orange peel effect showing through on the tights and gasp in horror. All the coffee beans you rubbed into them thighs was of absolutely no use. You still have lards of the C word.

You change grimly into a tent top and boot-cut jeans and look at yourself in all three mirrors seeing that the shelf ledge of a butt has been draped over graciously, the waistline is smoothened out under folds of fabric, and the jeans gently flare out at the bottom, balancing the width at the hip, giving you a silhouette of respectable proportions. You realise you are just an inch away from morphing into one of the kurti brigade and shudder in horror at how the mighty have fallen. There was once a phase when the T-shirts had to be second skin and you needed help to get out of them.

I hope the child realises the sacrifices one has made for his appearance on this earth. The multiple stomachs. The year spent being a milch cow. The career given up to be a stay-at-home mom. Gah.

Anyway. Suffice to say I am not a woman who travels light. I have been known to go on a trek with three lipsticks and foundation in my backpack. And I have been known to use them to refresh my appearance mid-trek. Needless to say, I decided that trekking wasn't really my cup of tea once I landed at the damn table-top of the mountain, bruised, sore and burnt to cinder. I have since stayed off anything that requires physical activity in sunny climatic conditions. Making the sole annual exception of running the parents' race at the child's Sports Day and unfailingly coming last in the event.

Coming back to the present, we were to spend a night and a day in a cottage in Lonavla, accompanied by a couple whom we thankfully both enjoyed the company of. And their son, who was a year younger than Kabir, whom he loved bossing over in the authoritative kind of way children have when God gives them a child younger than them to be bossed around for the duration of a few days with no escape. Needless to say, I was often glad that Kabir had no younger sibling when I watched him in action with the child in question.

The brat was dosed with half an Avomine duly powdered, and put into the back seat to sleep the journey out in peace. I am so tempted to use Avomine some nights when he keeps bouncing off the walls until well past the witching hour. I can divide travel sagas into pre-Avomine and post-Avomine eras. The pre-Avomine era included a lot of backseat whining about whether we've reached starting about five minutes after leaving home, insistence on being fed burgers at every McDonald's one passed on the way, and finally, the heaving up of all said burgers at regular intervals so that the interior of the car smelt like L'Eau de Barf for well into the next year despite manic shampooing and vacuuming.

The post-Avomine era included the child putting the head down on the seat and drifting off into a deep, dreamless sleep for hours, waking up only when one is turning into the hotel/resort/cottage and the worst of the journey is behind us. I want to go down on bended knee and thank the good soul who put together this formulation. I think he deserves a Nobel Prize in Medicine at the very least. Has he been awarded one? I was always very ditzy on general knowledge, don't think I ever won a GK quiz in my life.

Kabir popped his head up occasionally, with the kind of drowsy effort that is not subdued by a longing for burgers to ask, if we had passed McDonald's yet, and on being reassured that the golden arches were yet a far way off, he snuggled back with his much-tattered stuffed doggie aka Doggie. The child was taking after his father in the matter of prosaicness. No poetry in his soul. No, if he was ever confronted with the glorious sight of the stars as a canopy on a moonless night he would ask me to switch the lights on.

We reached and disembarked, just as the other couple turned into the driveway in their car. I suddenly noticed how bristly my friend's husband was and immediately thought of Sheetal Jaiswal's husband. As we hugged and said our hellos, the kids began their slow dance of reacquainting themselves with each other. A ritualistic process that included a little friendly shoving to check the boundaries of how far they could go. The cottage by itself was a pleasant sight for the eyes, perched on a cliff with greenery around as far as the eye could see. A swimming pool that stretched out invitingly, considering the sun was still high up in the sky, and rooms that were well stocked and comfortable.

We bustled in with our suitcases and had the usual ritual of checking out the rooms and trying to angle the better ones for ourselves and then laughing and giving the children the right of choice, and then it all ending in bitter tears with the kids deciding they wanted a bedroom to themselves and for the four adults to share the only other bedroom. Finally, the debate was settled by watchman cum Man Friday who carried in the separate batches of bags from each car into respective rooms and gave us no option but to accept his allocation, which seemed immensely fair given that we were handed the room with the better view.

The kids had already emptied out their individual backpacks of their cannot-bear-to-live-without toys and were engaged in acts of violence and destruction, including dismembering action figures with great many whoops and squeals of joy.

And shrieks of protest. 'Mamma, Ravin is nod sharing hiz toyz wid me!' squealed the child in much agitation. 'Tell him, tell him to be a gud boy and share hiz toyz now.'

The Ravin in question gathered his toys to himself and held onto them grimly with a Don't Mess With Me Look in his eye and, we noticed, had gathered some of Kabir's toys as well into the fold. The paters decided to resolve the dispute by taking their offspring into the pool for a quick swim before settling down for some beer before lunch. We mothers sighed in relief and began doing girly things like channel-surfing and gossiping. Suman, Ravin's mother, is a college friend of mine married to Navin, who is a college friend of the spouse. Ergo, we find getaways together very congenial since each one has a comfort level with the other. And yes, the spouse and I were college sweethearts, in case you didn't guess. We passed each other by the first-floor banisters, and by the time we reached the second-floor common rooms, we had decided we would never be parted.

'Such a terrible business in your neighbourhood last weekend,' she moued. 'And to think you guys were the ones who found the second body!'

I shrugged vaguely, trying to sort out some niggling questions in my head, which niggled like only niggling questions in the head can niggle.

'What do you think it is? Is it a serial killer on the loose?' she asked, her delicate face creased into a question mark. Suman is the sort who speaks in inverted commas. Through our college days I envied her her pretty delicateness, and now I positively turned an ugly shade of Hulk neon green whenever I met her, given that my own not-so-delicate self had taken a sacred oath to spread in every single direction it could while she continued to shop happily in the children's and the teenager's sections.

Being petite had its disadvantages, she tried to tell me when I was in the mood to listen to the other side of the tale. 'You cannot find sexy clothes in your size!' I didn't buy that of course. 'You risk getting trampled in a crowd.' That I bought. 'The only shoes that fit me are Bubblegummers!'

'I don't know Su,' I replied. 'I'd asked Runa to come in on this, and she's found out that the lady was murdered by a junkie who stole a gold chain she was wearing. And that the chappie who we found was killed by someone powerful because he was blackmailing him.'

'That seems pretty solved, but it must be so horrible to live in an area where two murders have happened,' she continued. I nodded. My mind was distracted. It was nothing for her to take too much note of. My mind was often distracted. I had often been hauled over the coals in college for staring at the blackboard with an expression of total blankness. The kids squealed in terror outside the French glass windows—which I made a mental note to lock as soon as they re-entered the cottage—as their fathers dunked them into the pool.

'Runa seems to have a nose for these things,' Suman went on. Suman knew Runa through me. And what I reported to her about Runa. And the occasional times she had met Runa at my home for dinner.

We twiddled our toes for some time. I checked my UberTwitter for any interesting status updates I just had to respond to right now or die. Nothing of kill-me-now importance, except for the usual celebrity circus tweeting about the latest films being released. I returned to the moment.

'Do you think people who get killed become ghosts,' asked Suman, with the kind of naïveté that made me want to fling her right back to school days. We were grown women with children. It was not okay to believe in ghosts. And ghosts didn't exist. Or did they? I had sat through enough stories on my grandmother's knee in my childhood about incredibly beautiful women with feet turned the other way round, who hung around at water sources waiting for random men to be entranced by them so they could suck their souls out. Or the child who cried through the night in a strange house but could never be found. Or Sheetal Jaiswal looking at me mournfully from outside my French windows. Which, of course, I didn't think I should mention to Suman. Yet.

'That's a fabbo colour on your toes,' I said. 'Which one is it?'

'Chanel Melrose,' she replied, admiring the startling bubblegum pink on her digits. I surveyed my toes and fingers glumly, noticing the slight chipping of the carefully applied My Karma Red which I had bought not because I was particularly enamoured of the colour but because I had tripped over the witty name of this shade, and some other ones. Including the nude At First Sight, which generally made my nails look like they had been pulled off by some gruesome Chinese torture method and was thus used most sparingly. And the Pink Before You Leap, which was a motto for my life—the reason why I always ended up wearing pink on days when I had to take momentous decisions. Pink calms me down. Maybe it is a hangover from the crib when I was no doubt draped in pink thanks to the chromosomal selection process that resulted in me being a girl.

'I think I keep seeing the woman who was killed,' I confessed hastily to Suman to fill the gaping hole in the conversation which had just happened. I hate holes in a conversation. I feel compelled to rush in and stuff whatever I can just to plug them. I have been known to start rambling on about the weather just because I felt uneasy about the silence at a marketing conference dinner back in the days when I pulled on formal work-wear every morning and caught the 8.24 a.m. into Churchgate station.

'You're kidding me?' she said, her little eyes widening into the kind of look that the blonde college girl generally gets when she sees the axe murderer advancing on her with saliva dribbling down his jaws.

'Nope, I'm not,' I moaned. 'I saw her in my balcony a night after the murder. I thought I spotted her on the road when I was jogging down that way. I even think I saw her standing in her balcony. And every time she seems to be looking at me in a very mournful manner.' Not that, I wanted to add, she was any cheerier when alive. In fact, her expression was perennially mournful. What did I really know about her, except where she lived and where she had died, and that she had a really bad-mannered husband. Maybe living with such a grouch would result in the perennially mournful expression.

Suman's eyes had now widened to worrying saucer-type levels. 'You're kidding me?' she repeated again. Though I love this girl, she has a vocabulary that would stretch across a single clothesline.

'No I'm not,' I replied, quite offended that I was being accused of being a fraud. 'And I'm not hallucinating either, clear as day I saw her standing, just looking at me. It freaked me out.'

'Why is she haunting you?' asked Suman. A question I had asked myself one time too many and couldn't find the answer to quite yet.

'Maybe,' I hazarded a guess, 'because I was the last person to see her alive.'

'Have you spoken to someone who knows about these things, you know ghost stuff?'

'No,' I replied. 'I haven't even told my hubby about it. He's the practical, sensible sort; he would just laugh in my face, and tell me to go sleep it off. You know.'

She sighed. Her husband had been baked in a similar mould. 'Yes, I know,' she replied, casting a loaded glance out at the pool area where the kids and the fathers were out of the pool shaking themselves down like dogs.

The children threw themselves into the living room wrapped in towels, their faces reddened by the sun. 'Hungry, hungry,' they squealed in rare unison on the issue. We asked for lunch to be served for the kids, and sat back with our Breezers, Cranberry and Orange if you must know, while the husbands lay back on shaded deckchairs and sipped their beers in the rare spirit of lazy bonhomie that a swim followed by a beer generally induces.

The kids fed, and threatened grimly into taking afternoon naps, we went across to join the men. The discussion was stubbornly stuck to things like property investments and prices, with the spouse moaning about the undoubted devaluation of the residence now that the area seemed to have become a murder and corpse-dumping ground.

'I've been trying to find out stuff about the Sheetal Jaiswal case,' I said, 'and apparently the police think some druggie killed her and stole her chain, while the other guy had some other reason that got him done in.'

The husband raised a sardonic eyebrow. 'And pray why are you getting yourself involved in all this? Let the police do their work, Kay, please. Murder is dangerous business. This is not something that is up your alley.'

I bristled as much as I could bristle while in reclining posture on deckchair with an Orange Breezer in my hand, which I was guzzling down in complete non-lady-like manner. I hmmmpphed. And harrumphed. And looked at the man with a scathing eye, which completely glanced off his carapace of complete indifference.

# CHAPTER 11

# IN WHICH WE RETURN TO THE CITY AND FIND THE CASES SOLVED

**W**E DROVE BACK OUT TO **M**UMBAI POST A heavy lunch the next day. The expressway was crisp and quick, and gleaming to the naked eye under the merciless December sun, and we found ourselves driving through our non-pearly gates within a couple of hours. We had already hugged and said our bye-byes at Lonavala itself since we were driving off in separate cars, and the kids had to be torn apart cruelly, sobbing to be allowed to sit together in the backseat of the car, something neither parent group was willing to accommodate given the likelihood that the camaraderie would dissipate into bloodcurdling yells and punches to the head and the stomach.

There was a buzz around the normally quiet road our complex is at the end of. The turn-off to the complex saw the police van, now ubiquitous, with some activity happening within and without that made me stick my neck up like a meerkat as we approached. Meerkats? Know them? You haven't been watching Animal Planet, have you? They have one meerkat among the clan who is generally on watch, and he (or she) is a sight to behold, standing on hind feet, sniffing the air, neck craned in every direction to watch out for approaching predators. So thus it was that I stuck my head up. I saw Swarthy standing near the van; the husband did too. We stopped as we neared.

I got out of the car; the child was thankfully still knocked out with Avomine and did not need a restraining order on bounding out and entering the police van and asking policemen whether he could hold their weapons.

'Any news, sir?' I asked. Politely. The husband followed me quickly, ready to extricate me if I managed to get myself into any trouble.

'Madam,' he began, in a tone that seemed joyous, 'we have found the murderer of the lady from your complex. One of these drug-addict types. He robbed her gold chain and has confessed to the crime. He is in lock-up now, announce bhi kar diya media ko. Abhi channels par aa raha hoga. Kal paper mein ayega.'

As I said before, it did seem too cut-and-dried.

'And what about Rohit Sharma, the one who was shot dead?' I asked. I knew what he was going to say, but still needed to hear it from an official source.

'That is different murrderrr. That is contract killing. Supari. We know who the killer is, but abhi arrest karna baaki hai. We have the man who ordered the killing in custody. Thoda complicated baat hai,' he said with a sudden reticence, given the delicacy of the topic, I guessed.

He puffed out his chest a bit in pride, reminding me of a rooster swaggering around in a barnyard. 'Abhi, we have been ordered to do patrolling on this road, every four hours in the night and twice in the day.'

Which was fortunate, given that the road was generally deserted enough to have couples park their cars along the periphery and indulge in some nooky causing windows to steam up and such like. I'm sure the couples who populated the vicinity would have cruel and harsh words for the murderers, for depriving them of one of the few last spots in this uncaring city where people in love and lust could retreat to for, err, recreation.

I reached home to the intercom ringing off its hook with folks wanting to discuss the findings of the police which they had already intimated to the society chairman and secretary, and which naturally, given the nature of such news, had already dissipated far and wide into the recesses of the community, so that even the elderly grouch who emerged only once a year for the Independence Day flag-hoisting celebrations was lurking around in the building lobby while the men and occasional women folk discussed vital issues like forming an ALM and hiring additional security to patrol the streets fringing the complex through the night and early morning.

'Kanan,' hissed Raji into the phone, 'did I tell you there's a woman in Sheetal Jaiswal's home?'

Hadn't she told me this before? Hadn't I seen him standing with a woman in the balcony a few days ago?

My ears cocked up. If I were a dog, they would standing upright, alert, in that kind of look dogs get when they have sniffed that something of chase and mangle proportions is in the near vicinity. If I were a tracking animal, I would have bounded right now in search of my prey.

'She could be a relative? A sister?' I hissed right back, wondering whether it was the need of the moment to sniff something rotten in the house of Jaiswal.

'No! My top work maid told me there's definitely something going on between them,' she hissed back. 'She works there at his house too na!'

A tube light switched itself on in the dim dark recesses of my mind and illuminated every nook and every corner. 'Raji,' I said in normal tone of voice, 'first of all, let us stop this whispering. No one is listening in to our conversation. And secondly, let's have a chat with your maid, is she around now?'

'Of course not,' Raji replied in the kind of tone that clearly indicated my brains had been taken out to the cleaners and had not yet been deposited back in my cranium. 'It is seven in the evening now. She will come in tomorrow morning; we could speak with her then.'

'No mobile?' I asked. In this era where every maid and cook and driver marched around cooing and billing into their mobile handsets, a maid without a mobile was like meeting a teenage girl without an eating disorder.

'No mobile,' she replied. 'I'm sure she has one, but I bet she switches it off when she comes to my place, so that she doesn't need to give me the number. They're very clever, these maids. They want to be able to bunk without us having any means of reaching them, and who on earth will go into the slums to hunt them down.'

The entire rear end of the complex we lived in was one massive residential area for the construction workers on the multiple towers coming up all over the place like Lex Luther's crystal city. Their wives were the ones who generally made it into the hallowed residential complexes as day maids. And most of them were illegal immigrants and therefore on the lookout for any opportunity to get into the system, which included getting ration cards and PAN cards made, even if they had no specific income which merited getting said PAN cards made.

I asked Jamuna if she knew the woman who worked at Raji's. There is one cardinal rule for every woman trying to run a house with maids: never underestimate the maid network. If you mistreat a maid, word will get round faster than you can blink and you can rest assured that you will have to import a maid from an agency or from your village because none of the locals will want to work at your place for love or money.

So of course Jamuna knew Raji's maid. She informed me of the extent she knew her, including little-known facts about her personal life involving an alcoholic husband and a young stud driver lover. Whom I declined to get further details about, because, frankly, the maid's personal life was not being discussed. It was the man she worked for that I needed more information on.

Apparently Jamuna and Raji's maid had become rather thick pals through evenings spent supervising our respective children in the park, discussing complicated issues like salaries and perks and Diwali bonuses, as well as how to tackle the romantic advances from the various cleaners, security guards and drivers populating the premises. There were entire romantic sagas being enacted in our premises right under our noses, which I chose to ignore unless Jamuna was down with a bad case of the broken heart, and needless to say, I kept greater tabs on the arrival of her menstrual cycle than I did of my own. She promptly fished out her little mobile decorated with beads on a tassel and jabbed a few buttons with practiced ease.

'Hullo? Malti? Main bol rahin hoon. Jamuna,' she reeled off. There seemed to be some memory block which prevented Malti from recalling Jamuna, and so she set about giving a detailed physical description of herself in terms so glowing that I had to look at her again to correlate the description with the person standing in front of me.

'Mere madam ko terese baat karne hai,' she said finally, and plonked the instrument into my hands.

I am not the best person to ask questions. Or draw out people. I am the kind of investigator who, had I been in police service, would sit through a serial killer lying his way through a questioning and then let him go because it felt rude to question him or refute what he'd said. 'Aap Sheetal madam ke ghar mein kaam karte hain? Jiska khoon ho gaya tha?' I asked tentatively.

'Haan, haan. Two years se,' she replied, breaking into English, probably to inform me that she was not a regular top work maid, but one who also spoke English and therefore was more desirable in the hiring sweepstakes.

'Kya aap abhi mere ghar par aa sakte ho?' I asked her, knowing that her home was probably a jump away. 'Bahut zaroori kaam hai.'

She hemmed and hawed in the way that folks who have no real immediate task at hand do, but finally agreed to come over.

In fifteen minutes the doorbell rang and Jamuna opened the door to her. 'Bhabbhhhhiiiii . . . Bhhhabbbbhi . . .' yelled Jamuna from the main door, in tones loud enough to wake the dead slumbering in the graveyard outside the church in the next suburb.

Malti was of the thin frame that some women who work as housemaids possess. If she had to be calibrated with a body fat calliper, she would show zero body fat. I wanted to go down on bended knee and ask her to sign up as my personal trainer. I thought woefully of my own love handles with sorrow, drew my wrap closer to my corpus colossus and wondered if doing the sweeping and swabbing would get rid of the excess corpulence which had swiftly deposited itself on my midsection and my rear. She draped herself at the doorjamb with a kind of limpidness that almost had me sending for the mop in case she dissolved into a puddle at my feet.

I asked her a few leading questions in a casual manner, not wanting to show my greed for information before leading up to the big question about the woman in Sheetal Jaiswal's flat. Currently hanging around there, and presumably up to no good with Bristly. A nail scratched up a blackboard in my head at the very thought. I resolved to haunt the spouse in true Poltergeist fashion if he dared to bring in a substitute for me so swiftly after I'd taken off for heavenly climes. If I did take off for heavenly climes before he did.

Malti was eager to spill the beans though. She had mentioned this to Raji in passing, she mentioned. And she repeated it now for my benefit. The husband and wife, I was told, were at constant loggerheads. The husband did no constructive work except lose money on ill thought-out business ventures, funded by the wife, who evidently came from a well-to-do family, but had married said bearded one for love. The love wasn't too much in evidence in recent times, according to Malti, who swore on all that was holy and on her mother's head that the man had been asked to leave the premises by Sheetal, who owned the flat they lived in, it having been gifted to her by her parents and it being in her name. They had no offspring. And, Malti hissed, only the good Lord above being privy to how she had landed upon such information, they didn't have marital relations anymore for any offspring to be possible.

'They would have such terrible fights, Madam,' she told me, her eyes widening in embellishment, 'throw this, throw that, and at the end of it, I would slip out quietly before they decided to start throwing things at me for a change.'

She hissed about the possibility of there being another woman in the man's life. 'Pata nahin Madam, aaj kal a lady keeps visiting. I never saw her come before, when Sheetal bhabhi was alive. Pata nahin kaun hai.' Bristly had, she said, emptied out all Sheetal's clothes the very next day after she had died. Put them in three huge black garbage bags and placed them outside the door for the housekeeping staff to take away. And even calmly signed the out voucher for the bags when one of the housekeeping chappies requested it so that he could take said disposed clothes and hawk them in the second-hand clothes market that ran near the railway station. Uncharacteristic of a man who should be mourning a recently deceased-under-very-brutal circumstances wife.

It all got curiouser and curiouser. I wondered if I should call Runa with these latest developments, but decided to wing it alone.

Malti had been questioned by the police, she said. But she had held onto all information related to marital conflicts, uncertain whether she would get into trouble with Bristly for having revealed more than was essential for a maid to reveal.

I decided to trot down and check if Swarthy was still hovering around the police van or whether he had taken himself and the van off to the police station. Luckily he was still there, and I seized the moment with a boldness I did not know I possessed and unburdened my suspicions to his puzzled countenance.

'But we have a murderer with a confession,' he squawked. 'Panchnama, FIR is filed!' I insisted he interview the spouse one last time, and with the luck of the bold, he agreed. He disappeared into the van and did some speaking into the wireless which I couldn't comprehend. I had visions of him calling for a SWAT team back-up which would take up sniper positions in the garden and the lobby to shoot down Bristly should he dare try to make an escape, and decided that I needed to cut down on the blood and gore movies. Swarthy strode with as dignified a stride as his uniform could give him, through the wrought iron black gates of the complex, taking himself rapidly towards the E wing of the complex.

As I moved back to the lobby of the tower I lived in, I saw a small tempo with some straggly bits of furniture being unloaded and a familiar back, minus the Velvet Smoking Jacket, overseeing the proceedings. I gasped. Audibly. If I could, I would have kicked myself soundly on the behind for said audible gasp. The back turned and the man faced me. This was my cue to say something extremely woman-of-the-world like. 'Fancy seeing you here,' or something to that effect, but all that came to the throat was a goldfish-like glug, and the awareness that I was in ratty tracks and faded T-shirt with the logo of a telecommunications service provider which had done quite an effective advertising campaign involving a pug which did things that were not humanly possible like sit still and lick stamps instead of doing what any rational dog would do, i.e., raise a leg to all the piles of sealed envelopes and spray them with what dogs dispense around freely to mark their territory.

I glugged and shrank back into the shadows, hoping I hadn't been recognised. Too late. He came up to me, smiling wide enough to make a rictus face. 'And we meet again . . .' he drawled.

I nodded, in what I hoped was a gracious fashion. Most likely I looked like there was a crick in my neck I was trying to ease. 'Are you moving in today?' I asked, and kicked myself on the mental shin for making such terrible conversation.

'Yes, I hardly have any stuff, but whatever I have goes into the house today,' he said. Seeming terribly happy about it.

'Err, do you live alone?' I asked, and then took the whips out to my back mentally.

'Yes, I do,' he smiled. 'My parents come down occasionally for a month or so from Ludhiana, but it's mainly me on my own. And I needed to move out of my previous apartment, something unpleasant happened there.' I nodded politely, trying to figure out how to end the conversation without seeming too rude. After all, one needed to be neighbourly now, and if I was anything I was neighbourly. 'My flatmate just got murdered last week,' he continued. 'He was found just on the road behind this complex, you know, last week.'

I gasped. My jaw yawned. My eyes goggled. I managed to get the mandibles back to position to articulate, 'Rohit Sharma?'

He nodded, lips twisting into a thin grin, almost as if we had managed to connect through MBA batchmates. This was what was called Coincidence. A Fluke. Whatever.

I remembered what I had heard of the deceased Mr Sharma via Runa, and did a narrow-eyed once-over of the specimen in front of me, standing carefully to the side while the moving men heave ho-ed random bits of furniture down. I noticed for the first time that the Velvet Smoking Jacket wore coordinated shoes and socks, and his eyebrows seemed too tidy to be of the untouched by thread version.

'Errr, no, no, no . . .' he began, noticing the sudden quizzical look that had infiltrated my prejudiced eye. 'We were just flatmates, you know, just moved into the city from same small town, and the rents here are so terribly high.' I continued to examine him head-to-toe with my non-existent gay-dar and came to no conclusion, except that I had to ask him where he'd got those ash blonde and chestnut highlights put in. Done very skilfully, I had to admit. Gah.

Just then the effervescent Mrs Kapur passed by with her Pomeranian and squealed in delight as she spotted Velvet Smoking Jacket. She picked up as much pace as her arthritic knees would allow and bore down on him like a ship approaching a tug boat. 'Arrey! Veer! Aapko dekh kar bahut khushi mili,' And insisted on showering him with her blessings. I looked on perplexed as Velvet Smoking Jacket, now of course clad more reasonably in a white cotton T-shirt and blue ripped jeans, simpered appropriately and told her how it meant so much that people like her appreciated his work, and I gathered through the conversation that he was, in fact, like half the population in my building complex, of the breed called TV actors. And within the two clear divisions in which TV actors seem to be categorised, namely the good guys and the bad guys, he was safely ensconced in the good-guy category, which meant that none of the elderly women around were likely to try and stab him with their agarbattis for inflicting woe and misery on their favourite tortured female character, aka a long-suffering bahu.

Veer? Hmm. So that was the Velvet Smoking Jacket's name. Was that his real name or his small screen name, I wondered.

I stood around determined to continue the small talk, with all the finesse and delicacy of a monkey ferreting out the ants from an ant hill, never mind if Mrs Kapur was around to be party to the conversation. I needed to ask him about Rohit Sharma, about why he thought his flatmate had been decimated by a bullet to his brain. I wondered why he was moving out of his old flat in such a hurry. I wondered whether he had been the slender, well-manicured hand that had pumped the slug into the brain of the deceased Mr Sharma; a lover's tiff perhaps? I was bubbling over with questions, and the hand was itching to speed dial Runa with this latest development, which undoubtedly would be key to our investigation. I remembered he had been winking at me at parties while Rohit Sharma was being measured out lengthwise in the centre of the road for our unsuspecting car to almost drive over, but perhaps the supari killing wasn't as cut-and-dried as they made it out to be.

'You know,' I interjected into the laudatory conversation, physically moving myself so I could be in the foreground, having been unceremoniously shoved to the side by virtue of a yapping Pomeranian sniping at my ankles, 'I actually found his dead body, I and my husband. On the back road. We were coming back from that party, you know, you were at the party . . .'

'I know,' he said, face contorting in what seemed like a moment of pain. 'I found out he had been killed the next morning when the cops landed up at our flat asking questions.'

Mrs Kapur, dismayed at being excluded from the conversation, looked at each of our faces alternately like some spectator watching a long drawn-out tennis rally. Then realising she had nothing to contribute, she offered largesse in the form of a home-cooked dinner for the poor boy, living alone without his parents, facts she had not gleaned from this conversation so had undoubtedly scrounged off some television star snippet column in the dailies, and then drifted homewards.

To return to the conversation where we left it. The flat. Why the hurry to move out, I asked aloud. 'The lease had run out,' he said disarmingly. 'And now I'm doing fairly well so I don't really need to share. Anyway, there were too much problems with Rohit, all the time.' He lowered his voice, 'He wanted to get into films, he was too ambitious. He got mixed up with the wrong people.'

I practically salivated at the information I could extract from him if only I knew how to. I needed to get Runa here, now. I scuffed at the paving stone underfoot and mumbled something about catching up with him soon, and how he was free to call on the intercom if he required anything.

'Anything?' he asked with a laconic raised eyebrow, making me morph immediately into a blithering bundle of adolescent nerves.

He was the flatmate of a man who wore purple satin shirts, I told myself sternly. I had no reason to be reduced to a bundle of adolescent nerves. 'Numbers of delivery stores, chemists and such like,' I clarified tartly and walked away, jabbing furiously at the phone to call Runa, only for it to go through to voicemail.

'Call me back,' I said after the tinny beep. 'There's been an interesting development in the Rohit Sharma case.'

In the lift with me was Mrs Manchanda from the twelfth floor, bubbling over with excitement like a teenage girl at having glimpsed a television star unloading his tempo full of furniture, and at the prospect of encountering television royalty in the lift every day. She would call her parlour girl across tomorrow morning, she stated. It wouldn't do to be caught unexpectedly in the premises with eyebrows resembling caterpillars, and arms giving credence to her affiliation to being part of the tribe of women who run with the wolves. She sighed twice. Deep and long. It was the sigh of a woman past her prime who knew that no matter what face pack was applied to her epidermis, it would not bring the roses back to her cheeks. I was long divorced from roses on said cheeks too, a minor problem solved by dreamy mousse Damson Rose blush which had me masquerading for a spring chicken whenever the need arose. And I was fine with faking it. No way was I going to down salads and healthy nutrition to get it all naturally. I am a faker. If anything could be faked, I would do it with a smile. Which included faking a headache.

This reminded me that I was overdue for a manicure and pedicure and some basic exfoliation, so we settled that the girl would visit Mrs Manchanda first and then she would send her to my place. Not that Velvet Smoking Jacket had influenced this decision in any way, mind you. My once-a-fortnight appointment with the little girl with the big bag who visited all the houses in the complex, at convenient afternoon timings, was fixed. She knew that alternate Friday afternoons were to be reserved for Kanan Mehra or Cain would be raised. So I didn't care whether or not I was presenting a defoliated visage to Velvet Smoking Jacket in the lift. It would help of course, if I didn't have whiskers on my upper lip to stroke at thoughtfully in the midst of conversation.

Which reminded me, the conversation in question needed to be completed. The intercom was dialled. 'Raji, who is this Veer person who has moved into the building. He acts in some serials.'

Raji's husband does something at a channel. Programming Head it is called. Ergo, she knows most of them television actors personally, gives one insider dope, and is pretty much your one-stop shop if you want to be part of television audience on any show from the channel. Not that I have taken her up on that very generous offer.

She gasped. 'Veer? Tall. Sharp nose? Nice eyes?' Yup. Pretty much summed him up, I agreed. 'Which rock are you under? He's the main lead in that serial where his girlfriend gets married to his best friend who treats her real bad and he mopes around the place until his mother gets him married to his girlfriend's best friend who is a bitch . . . .'

That could have been any serial, give or take one evil in-law. I interrupted. 'What's his real name?'

She thought for a while. 'Rana something.'

'Rana what?' I persisted. 'What?' My voice was going shrill. I gritted my teeth. I needed to know people by their full names. It was a sort of compulsion, like I filed them in my head, all alphabetically sorted.

She noticed the hard edge to my voice. 'Arrey, why is it so important, the name will come to me in a while. I'll call you when it does. Achcha, want to hit the Christmas sales at Primaverus?'

Did I want to? I would leave skid marks as I entered the mall. For now, I left it at that and checked with the security guard as to which flat the TV actor was moving into. 1602. Two floors below me. Bang opposite the retired Mr Bose, he of the firm and voluble opinion about service contractors fleecing the managing committee. Maybe I should saunter around and ask him some more about the dear recently departed. I wondered how I could deposit myself on his doorstep uninvited and start doing the third-degree on him, without the help of a naked bulb hung overhead or his hands tied behind his back.

I could be the welcoming neighbour and trot over with some roti-sabji-dal-chawal. Didn't them bachelor-types, far from maa ke haath ka khana weep like little babies when confronted with homemade food that was all theirs to eat? But then maybe he was on some macrobiotic diet like so many of them glamour-types, and the spoonfuls of ghee my cook flung into the tadka might just choke up his gullet and not get me any information. I decided to do it later. After all I was tired. I needed to get my eight hours of beauty sleep. Post a nutritious, calorific dinner of course.

I wondered whether I would see Sheetal Jaiswal again in the night. A cold chill ran up my spine, again, even though she had been a pretty non-threatening ghost till now. But then she was a ghost, right? A creature from another dimension. A lesser person than me would have peed her pants, I consoled myself. I had seen her and tried to figure out why it was that she was trying to contact me, and why was it that she didn't say anything. I shivered and walked into the bedroom, where the child promptly jumped at me to demand that dinner be Maggi Thrilling Curry with Chicken Nuggets. With Tang for liquid refreshment on the side. I wondered sadly what happened to the good old days when children ate what was placed before them and only dared revolt, that too a token revolt given our parents were such dragons, if said item of nutrition included such exciting options as the dreaded lauki and karela.

# CHAPTER 12

# IN WHICH ALL'S WELL THAT ENDS WELL

**F**OR SOME REASON, my lavender and patchouli essential oils infused eye mask failed to calm me down enough to drift into a state so soporific that only a bomb dropped on the building would be guaranteed to wake me up. Which it normally did manage to do every single day.

I found myself pushing said eye mask up at regular intervals and checking the time on the mobile I keep by my bedside. I looked out at the balcony, beyond the French windows, expecting to see a mournful Sheetal Jaiswal peering in at me, with a plea on her face, a plea I couldn't quite decipher. But then I can't decipher quite a number of things unless they are written out with black marker on a white board and held in front of me at a distance of approximately two feet.

The child was sprawled across the bed while the spouse and I huddled at the edges like the dispossessed, where one wrong turn would see us tumbling onto cold, unwelcoming tiling.

It was high time the child was definitively shunted into his own room. I needed to tourniquet my bleeding heart and firmly tuck him in and say my good nights. The spouse had been campaigning for this for many years now, for totally selfish reasons, and would do the chicken dance if it came through.

Anyway, Jamuna would be snoring in the same room, and would alert me if we were required, or to reassure him if he got up howling from a bad dream. And the spouse would wake up in the morning with a jaunty smile on his face, instead of moping around the premises like someone sucked all the joy out of his life and making pointed and unfairly cutting remarks about having been forced into celibacy despite being married, and a faithful husband. And about how he should dig out his little black book and dial some numbers, not knowing of course that his wife has long consigned said little black book to the flames over a gas stove and is pleased that he has not had occasion to notice its absence from the spot he normally stored it. He deserved the child to be shifted to the other room. That would be his reward, I decreed.

I set myself a mental deadline for the transition to happen within the next week. I would rope in the spouse, I told myself, to convince the child that he was now a big child, and said big children slept on their own without kicking their parents into insomnia through the night.

When the mosques at a distance began blaring out the morning azaans my eyes were still open. It was still, in child parlance, the dark morning, so I refused to raise my carcass off the bed, but wondered whether it would be worth my while to go down for a quick jog. Sleep won finally, and I drifted off to the synchronised snores of the spouse who definitely needs one of those nose tapes which reduce the decibel levels of said snoring, and the child who snores in the incredibly cute non-offensive way that children snore.

The doorbell and the clattering in the kitchen woke me up with a start. The clock showed 8.30 a.m. This was the latest I had slept in since the child had been removed through a precise surgical incision, which is now camouflaged at the bikini line under the slight overhang of tummy which exists to be the bane of my life.

I sprang to life and into the bathroom where the toothbrush beckoned me seductively. Morning dogbreath is so not a good way to start the day. I can slay with morning dogbreath. Maybe I should go for my morning jogs without brushing them teeth. I would be guaranteed of a weapon stronger and more powerful than any piddly can of pepper spray could ever be.

Jamuna, I could hear, was in deep and intense conversation with an indeterminate person at the door. I ventured out of the bedroom to investigate. The maid I'd spoken with yesterday, Malti, was draped at the door in her patented asparagus-like fashion. She informed us that the police were currently questioning Sheetal Jaiswal's husband and she had been asked by him to return in the afternoon to do her work. The thought that the information she had shared yesterday might have something to do with the reappearance of the police at his doorstep was making her hyperventilate.

'Mera naam nahin liya na, Madam!' she squawked. I poured on the reassurance thick that she was nowhere in the picture.

I was told there was a posse of policemen stationed at the gates of the building today. And some very stern questioning was going on. And everyone getting into and out of the premises was being asked to prove they were who they said they were, which had created a major problem for some residents who had marched out for their morning constitutionals without any proof of identification.

I picked up the Blackberry from the bedside table and called Runa. 'Kay!' she barked. 'Don't you have something better to do than wake me at 8.30 on a Sunday morning?'

I quaked. I thanked the good Lord that her beady eyes of pain were not focused on me. I quickly rattled off all that I had found out since the previous night and hastily disconnected the phone. Runa, if I knew her, would be bounding into the police station without even bothering to change out of her sleepwear. And no, it would not be a sight that would gladden the heart of any onlooker. It would be a sight that would make the man trawling matrimonial sites swear to eternal bachelorhood.

I discarded sleepwear in favour of more suitable raiments for a public airing and trotted off, metaphorically speaking, downstairs. The raiments, if you must know, were capris and a sleeveless blue cotton top which did nothing to enhance my munificent curves, but rather converged me into one humungous tree trunk of fat and therefore had been consigned to occasional, within the building complex wear.

True to report, the premises were swarming with khaki-clad ones. And the watchman whispered conspiratorially that they were about to arrest Mr Jaiswal. He had it on authority from the third constable to the right who had informed him of the same when he asked for the key to the common toilet for the security and the housekeeping staff. Murli floated around like only an odd-job man can and took it upon himself to inform me that, 'Ek bada saab aaya, pooliss ka bada saab.' The pooliss ka bada saab had stepped into the E wing at the ungodly hour of 7 a.m. And had not emerged since.

Was it worth hanging around the lobby to catch a glimpse of the man being led off in handcuffs? I wondered. Or should I go back home and down my mug of late morning tea and wake myself up as God mandated I should? Decisions, decisions. The tea won and I trotted back to the lobby. Where I found Rana Something aka Velvet Smoking Jacket aka Veer emerging from the lift directly in my face and ergo unavoidable. If I could have hopped behind a pillar I would, but I decided to gird my loins, metaphorically speaking, in order to take the self-delegated investigation forward. After all, I was the one who had barfed on discovering Mr Bullet in the Head. I owed it to Rohit Sharma.

'Hey there,' he raised a hand in a 'I Come In Peace' greeting made popular in noisy, crowded dance places where actual audible greeting is not possible. I smiled back, thanking my stars that fate had thrown us together in this manner and not required me to take myself to his doorstep in order to restart the thread of conversation from the previous day.

'Hello, just the person I wanted to meet,' I said, doing the seize-the-day thing as recommended by them group of poetic types who spoke of graves and virginity, and proceeded to block his path in most unladylike manner. 'I wanted to ask you a little bit about Rohit Sharma.'

He sighed dramatically, with the standard expression that he might be called upon to give when told the love of his life was being married off to the neighbourhood paan-chewing Lothario. 'What about him?'

'Who do you think killed him? Really?'

He looked around. Stroked his rather chiselled chin thoughtfully. He was a good actor. In the span of a couple of minutes, he had given me a plethora of expressions. If I were a casting director, I would have hired him NOW. Without the couch, of course.

'There are two theories, which one do you want?'

I never claimed to be a good girl who could pick one sweet and pass the plate on. 'Both, of course.'

He sighed. Dramatically. Ran a weary hand over his eyes. 'One theory says he was bumped off by his hot-shot producer-boyfriend, because he was blackmailing him.'

He looked keenly at me to check for shock value. Boyfriends having boyfriends and murders don't shock me anymore. I remained sanguine. 'And the second theory?' I asked, with a calmness that almost made me want to go check my temperature and blood pressure levels now. This detective business was making me cool, composed and collected. I didn't feel like me.

'I suspected he was in the drug business. He did drop-offs. He got greedy. They bumped him off.'

Errm. My ears pricked up. This was a new one. 'A drug dealer? How do you know?'

'We shared a flat, remember, why do you think I was so keen to get out of there and get my own place?'

'Have you told the police this?' I asked, wondering whether this was old hat or worth conveying to the Rune.

'The producer-boyfriend bit, yes, not the drug bit. I value my life. The next dead body on the road could be mine. By the way,' he said, extending a slender manicured hand, 'I am Rana Singh, and I don't have the pleasure of knowing your name.' It was the kind of old-fashioned self-introduction that I would have expected from someone twice his age, ah, he was an old soul in a young body. Next, he would be baring fangs and shinning up tall trees in the blink of an eye, and taking off to the nearby Yeoor Hills to feed on available wildlife. Of course, I'm kidding.

I shook his hand. Not too vigorously. It was the cold-fish kind of handshake that has one wipe one's palm surreptitiously against one's trouser after disengagement to rid oneself of the clammy feeling.

I smiled. And was acutely conscious that my smile wasn't quite reaching my eyes. Maybe this is was the best alternative to getting Botox injected into them spiderwebs making their presence felt around the eyes.

'Hi Rana,' I replied, in the most polite tones, 'you can call me Kay.'

'Kay?' he replied, sounded puzzled. Kay wasn't even a name. It was half a name. But it trips off the tongue so much easier than Kanan does.

'It's what my friends call me.'

Just then I spotted Swarthy striding past the building and I trotted after him, with a quick wave to Rana aka Veer. 'Sir, sir, bhau, bhau,' I yelled, causing him to stop in his tracks so suddenly I almost careened into his back.

'Ho Madam, kay pahije?' he asked, his face splitting into unequal halves with a grin exposing teeth of an extremely bilirubineque predisposition, speckled with a flagrant red evidencing a predilection of that horror called 'paan' which has unwary visitors to the country wince at the 'blood stains' spattered on every public surface.

Reverting to the national language, I said, 'I just wanted to know if you had been able to question Mr Jaiswal.' My voice was not commanding enough, I knew it as the sound waves left the mouth. Runa, in my place, would have fixed him with a beady stare and commanded him to sing out all he knew. Me, on the other hand, he dismissed as readily as an errant mosquito.

He laughed heartily. 'Wohi sab chal raha hai Madam . . . thoda patience rakho.'

Suitably put in my place despite all my pretensions to being a private investigator in training, I tucked my long chin into my belt and went back up home. There lunch plans were being made by the spouse and the child, and considering the fact that these plans involved a restaurant, I immediately perked up and got myself sparkling and dressed, and completely planning out what I was going to order for myself once I reached said restaurant and wondering why restaurants didn't as a rule have calorie counts of the items on their menus right next to where their prices were. I would read the right hand column with much more interest than I did currently.

So anyway, here we were, with me seriously attacking my plate with the kind of expression that brooks no conversation, with the spouse lazily on his second beer, and the brat insisting that he wanted only a McDonald's burger right now, when the phone rang. Runa. 'Hello,' I answered in strange voice, having gulped an unchewed morsel in order to respond at the earliest possible.

'Are you choking?' barked Runa. 'Sip on some water.'

'No, I'm fine,' I gulped. I knew without having to look in a mirror that my expression was goldfish-like. I often have an expression that is goldfish-like. It comes from me not comprehending what is going on around me, and it is the cue for some kind soul to come in and rescue me from putting my foot, manicured toes and all, right into my mouth.

'What's up?' I asked, wondering whether this could be a social call. Knowing Runa, it definitely wasn't. The hastily swallowed piece of fish peri peri stuck in my gullet was making my voice squeakier than it anyway became under natural circumstances when I entered into conversation with Runa.

'Guess what the police have? A confession from the junkie they arrested for your Sheetal Jaiswal's murder that he was paid to kill her. By her husband. Would you have believed it? He used to do odd jobs for her husband. They're arresting him right now, as we speak!' Her voice sounded jubilant. And conciliatory. 'You were right, you know. The case wasn't so cut-and-dried as it seemed. It was a valid point you made about the iPod.'

And that explained why Sheetal hadn't screamed in ear-piecing decibel tones for help when she came across him in the dark of the morning. She probably barely caught sight of the blade before it made contact with flesh. I sighed. And added my information gleaned from Rana the Veer for Runa's consideration. 'So, what do you think, Runa?'

'That case is closed Kay. And that has powerful people involved. I'm not touching it now . . .' she sounded uncertain. For Runa to sound uncertain about getting involved with something meant I needed to scoot out of whatever that something was, and leave skidmarks. Ergo, the case was closed for me too. I could just visualise solemn men with ghodas tucked into their belts breaking down my front door and putting a bullet through my brain should I be asking too many uncomfortable questions. And anyway, what goes of my father's, to translate the colloquial idiom into the Queen's English. It wasn't like I even knew the bullet-headed one.

She elaborated on the Sheetal Jaiswal story. It was scarily simple. The flat was in Sheetal Jaiswal's name, bought for her by her parents. The couple had fallen out of love. The man wanted to marry another woman, but didn't want to be thrown out onto the streets with his new beloved. The easiest option was to exterminate the old one, and the property would then naturally get transferred to him, being the legally-wedded husband and suchlike.

The man handed charge of the razor used to slit the lady's throat was to be paid Rs 50,000 in order to dispatch Mrs Jaiswal from her earthly corpus to the realm of eternal diets. He had pocketed half the advance, already had a criminal record for petty robbery and was on his way to collect his balance payment when he had been picked up by the police instead. First murder novice, he'd hawked the thin gold necklace he painstakingly ripped off Sheetal's neck and had the local jeweller in the neighbourhood reporting the transaction to the police after the news appeared in the dailies, in either a spirit of good citizenship or in terror of the ghost of Sheetal Jaiswal demanding her chain back, or more likely, a friendly visit from the local police asking about suspicious gold chains being hawked for immediate cash purposes. And the pink shoes did him in. The jeweller had noticed and remarked on the pink shoes. The moral of the story should be that never wear what you filch off a person you murder. He sang out information about the mastermind behind what seemed to be random robbery-turned-killing when promised a fix after two days of being locked-up cold turkey.

Interestingly, the recently bereaved Mr Jaiswal had already initiated documentation with the society to figure out the proceedings to transfer the flat into his name legally, and the unseemly haste of it all had caused some concerned committee members to mention the same to the investigating officers in the course of routine investigation.

I wondered whether Sheetal Jaiswal had been foolish enough to not make out a will. Have I spoken about the absolute importance of everyone making out a will, even if they think they're going to do the chicken dance at their hundredth birthday celebrations? No? Well now is not the time to talk about it.

I thought about Sheetal Jaiswal all the way home, which was a five-minute drive away after I was helped to my feet by two of the serving staff who pulled and heaved, and mopped their brows of the rivulets of sweat pouring down from the exertion. Okay, I exaggerate. I made it to the car on my own steam, and wanted to do nothing but crash out on my bed and snore in most inelegant fashion, post such indecent levels of gluttony. I knew though, that now that the murderer had been found to be a person within our own, there would be hullabaloo in the complex. There would be excited people bounding about in the lobby wanting to discuss the latest developments. These were developments that merited prompt analysis and postmortems and were not likely to be reserved for later.

I was not far off the mark. When we reached, practically the entire population of the complex, including a few Outstanding and Respected Members of the Society, were gathered gravely in the parking area, huddled together like a football team just about to run off onto field to decimate the opposition. The spouse was spotted and called in to join the huddle. I happily scampered off, needing, I told myself, at least ten minutes of shut-eye before I could even dream of entering any rational conversation. I saw the spouse being sucked into the discussion much like a morsel of tasty diver disappears into the gaping jaws of a great white.

The pater called. His tone was grim, like he was announcing a death and needed me to be brave. 'Kay *beta*, your brother is getting married. To a foreigner. And he tells us now, at the last minute, so I cannot cancel my Bandhavgarh trip to attend his wedding.'

I squealed in delight, much to his clucking disapproval. 'Anyway, speak with him and get the details,' he concluded after informing me the 'girl' in question was a thirty-two-year-old research analyst and the younger sibling and she were trotting off to the registrar's in a couple of weeks, after which they planned a 'get to know the in-laws' stop-over before whizzing off to Bali for their honeymoon.

Trust the brother to keep things hush even with me, not that we were too close given he had practically lived his entire life in a hostel having been shunted off to them infernal places since the time he was eight.

The mater, I was told, had taken to her bed with the shock and was in no condition to conduct a coherent conversation.

'Don't worry *beta*, once she realises having a *firangi bahu* is a status symbol in her kitty circles, she will be back to normal,' the pater assured me, having seemingly accepted that his son would now perhaps never return to the mother ship. 'I need to plan for a simple reception at the club when they're down in India,' he stated; after all, social obligations had to be met, or he wouldn't be able to show his face in public.

'You should come down when they're here. Last week of January, they're saying.'

My brother's wedding reception. A chance to bling myself to obscene, put-on-the-sunglasses levels. It had been a while since I'd done that at my own wedding. My brain lit up with a 1000-watt bulb. Shopping. I had an official reason to run shrieking into the malls and pick up a few new raiments of the ethnic formal variety. There was this darling chiffon saree with interesting embroidery down the pallav paired with a gold corset that had been calling out my name from the latest issue of the *Vogue*. I must hunt it down, or get a rip-off made by my local Mehta tailor, who, I swore on all that was holy, could have any of them fashion week designer-types stab themselves with a needle to a slow draining death should they know the price at which he manufactured exact replicas of what they retailed at rates that could feed a small family for a year.

I did what was expected of me and called the fraternal sibling to offer my congratulations and also to berate him soundly for keeping secrets about such life-changing decisions.

'Kay di,' he said, sounding chirpier than I'd heard him since he'd been in a fight in Class 6 and returned nose-bloodied, glowing with the pride of having knocked out a formidable ninth grader and his front tooth, 'I had to be sure before I told you guys. I hadn't even formally proposed to her yet. Rosanne, she is, and will mail you everything. Am just stepping out now.'

The heart was warm and fuzzy at the thought of the brother 'settling down' in the best tradition of tea leaves, and the body was drowsy with the lethargy brought on by gluttony. The child and I sprawled on the bed, the child in imitative appreciation of my lack of motion, me in true sleepiness brought on by overeating and the lack of sleep through the night. Jamuna was instructed not to disturb me unless there was need for immediate evacuation of the building. She nodded the kind of nod she has when she values her life and limbs.

'Phone aaya toh?' she asked warily.

'Take a message,' I replied.

'Urgent bola to?' she persisted with the kind of attention to detail which has me pleased should she choose to use it to get that last bit of grime out from behind the door in the cabinet beneath the bathroom sink.

'Saab ka number de do,' I replied in the kind of tone which brooked no further conversation. But not to Jamuna.

'Saab ne nahin uthaya to?' she went on.

I blew a mini fuse and did some yelling, and ended with closing the door hard and loud, and had the effect quite ruined with the child pushing the door open the next second and asking me to hop and shaoud laoudly agin so he could call his frens to watch. This child was born to be in the entertainment business as a wheeler and dealer, I just knew it.

He was given the raised eyebrow and took himself off to his room to play, having sensibly dropped the idea of selling tickets to ringside seats for the performance of 'Mom Throws A Tantrum'.

I slept a deep dark sleep which had me running through dark roads with the street lights flickering eerily, and seeing a shadow at the end of one road waiting for me, beckoning me to come near, and I move in, unable to resist or stay away, the voice as is normal in such kind of dreams had gone AWOL. As I close in, I see it is Sheetal Jaiswal, and she no longer looks sullen-faced. In fact, she smiles. And waves to me in a kind of cheery gesture that was made popular by Deepika Padukone in *Om Shanti Om*, and which looks infinitely better on a woman who is close to six feet tall and has the circumference of a ball point pen. She takes off on a run, looking over her shoulder at me, in true horror film fashion, hoping to lead me into dark, unmentionable realms where surely daemons with vats of boiling oil are lying in wait for unsuspecting me to come across, so they can feed me malai boti kabab until I can never bear to look at one again for the rest of my life. I try following her but she disappears so swiftly that I have no chance of catching up.

I woke up with the kind of start that leads me to feel I've experienced something surreal. And look beside me to see the child actually sleeping wide-mouthed enough for stray flying insects to investigate the interiors of his mouth and emerge unscathed. Which was surreal in itself, because this is after all a child who never naps in the afternoon come hell or high water and can still bounce off the walls in the evening like he has springs embedded under his soles. Obviously, the lunch had got to him too.

A quick glance at the clock on the wall showed me it was barely an hour since I'd drifted off to sleep. The spouse hadn't yet returned from the presumably avid discussion going on downstairs about murderers in the society and how they could be evicted from the premises without causing too much scandal so as to affect property prices in the area. The sun was setting gently over the distant horizon, the nip of the evening breeze was floating into the room. Happy squeals of the kids running around in the park reached my ears. All was right with the world again. I stood in the balcony and looked down at the patch of green where little figures which seemed like black spots on coloured sticks darted around furiously. The swings were all occupied by the elderly who sat in bunches and discussed the rates of vegetables and maids with a ferocity that could power a nuclear fission unit if someone managed to figure out how one could harness speech and convert it into energy.

Life was good. I went into the kitchen to supervise what the sullen cook had decided to inflict on us this fine evening. One of the most distasteful tasks I have to do every single day is to plan the menu. The menu for breakfast, the menu for lunch, the menu for dinner. It is a draining business, this planning of menus. You need to factor in dishes which will appeal to both the males in the house, both being of varying age groups, and therefore with requirements which are very specific to each.

I barked out my instructions to tone done the spice for the child and up the spice for the man, and decided to chop up some salad myself. It was the zenith of my culinary skills. I chopped up vegetables with love for the spouse, since he is the only salad eater in the family. I am the queen of unhealthy eating, and of scrambled eggs. I can also, in a pinch, boil up a Maggi noodles meal and a Sunfeast Pasta, but beyond this cooking is alien territory to me. I'm a blot on Linda Goodman who suggested that Cancerian women are incredibly good housekeepers and cooks. Maybe the husband should have protested violently when it became increasingly evident that any breakfast cooked by me would have a half-fried egg as the main component. Accompanied by slices of bread. And maybe a glass of tetrapacked juice. What? What? What? It's a balanced meal. Carbohydrates. Protein. Vitamins. What more can a man want? But a cook was quickly called into the household and became a permanent fixture. And I was so relieved about being out of the kitchen and free to do things that kitchen duty would otherwise tie me down to that I never ever made the effort to get back into the kitchen, except in a supervisory capacity.

As I sliced the cucumbers, the carrots and tomatoes, I thought about my dream. I wondered what the dream meant. Did it mean the obvious, that Sheetal Jaiswal had finally left the building, and would not be staring at me moodily from darkened corners? Did it mean she had at last found justice? Somehow, it didn't scare me anymore, the thought that I was in some form of inadvertent communication with a spirit, a spirit of a person I hadn't even known too well while she was alive. Somehow, a curious bond had been forged with me. A tenuous bond that strangely didn't terrify me. If you had told me a fortnight ago that I would be seeing a ghost at regular intervals, I might have gone into cardiac arrest and become one myself. But now, it felt normal. But she hadn't been a threatening kind of a ghost. I might have even invited her over for a cuppa had I figured out how to communicate with her. I'm a friendly person that way. I don't discriminate between the living and the non-living.

I didn't think I would be seeing much of her anymore, though. I wasn't particularly relieved; I was just proud of myself for not hyperventilating whenever I'd spotted her. Maybe I might just win the bravery awards someday and be allowed to sit atop the elephant on the Republic Day parade. Never mind if I was a few decades too late for that.

I smiled. I spliced my finger with the knife, misjudging the distance between my finger and carrot and blood spewed in every conceivable direction. I screamed loud enough to wake the dead, and felt the world go black. Now if I could just conquer my squeamishness about blood.